The Fairy Tale

My eternal thanks to all who made this dream a reality.
For T.B. and M.C. for all their support.

And always, for Quinn.

Table of Contents 1

Chapter One	2	Chapter Sixteen	115
Chapter Two	8	Chapter Seventeen	128
Chapter Three	15	Chapter Eighteen	139
Chapter Four	21	Chapter Nineteen	147
Chapter Five	26	Chapter Twenty	154
Chapter Six	31	Chapter Twenty-One	163
Chapter Seven	35	Chapter Twenty-Two	172
Chapter Eight	42	Chapter Twenty-Three	181
Chapter Nine	50	Chapter Twenty-Four	192
Chapter Ten	58	Chapter Twenty-Five	199
Chapter Eleven	65	Chapter Twenty-Six	211
Chapter Twelve	72	Chapter Twenty-Seven	219
Chapter Thirteen	81	Chapter Twenty-Eight	226
Chapter Fourteen	91	Chapter Twenty-Nine	239
Chapter Fifteen	102	Chapter Thirty	252
		Epilogue	275

Chapter One

Prince Coriander rode across the open plains, his short curly blond hair bouncing in the breeze. The steed moved smoothly beneath him, their movements in practiced sync from years of riding together. The sun warmly lit his tanned skin, drawing forth beads of sweat. The passing air brought a coolness as it crept across him, carrying with it the faint scent of damp earth and wildflowers, a smell that always reminded him of childhood summers spent exploring these very plains. He could almost hear the distant laughter of his younger self, racing across the fields with a sense of freedom that seemed to elude him now. The memories stirred something bittersweet in his chest—how much had changed since then, how much he had changed. The air was different now, too, tinged with the scent of autumn, of things ending.

The light blue tunic he wore whipped casually in the wind, barely containing his well-toned physique. Despite the strength his body displayed, there was always an unspoken pressure to be more—to be the perfect prince, the flawless warrior, the ideal leader. The tall yellowed grass gently grazed the fine dark leather of his trousers, as if nature itself acknowledged his presence. The leaves of the few sparse trees scattered across the fields had begun to change, showing red and orange sporadically among the usual green, a reminder that time, like the seasons, moved relentlessly forward.

He pulled his horse into a slow trot, the beast's breath deep and appreciative beneath him. Coriander's deep blue eyes scrutinized the land ahead. The way beyond here became more hilly, flecked with outcroppings of rocks. Not too far away, he could make out the edge of the forest marking the boundary of his father's lands—*someday, his lands*, Coriander thought with a smile, though the weight of the crown felt heavier on his mind with each passing year. He could already feel the expectations of his father and the kingdom pressing down on him, like the tightening grip of a gauntlet he had yet to don. The freedom of these open plains, the simple joy of riding with the wind in his hair, was something he feared losing once he took on the full mantle of kingship. What kind of ruler would he be? Would he be remembered for his wisdom, his strength—or his failures? Coriander's smile wavered, but only for a moment. He pushed the thoughts away and urged his horse onward, letting the familiar rhythm of the ride soothe his restless mind.

He knew he shouldn't go too much farther, especially without an escort. Despite the army's best efforts, the forest was known to be infested with bandits and other brigands. It certainly wasn't safe for the young crown prince. He checked the sword mounted to the horse's tack, and it slid easily clear of the scabbard with a slight ring. The handle was warm and familiar in his hand, the leather worn to fit his grip perfectly. It was a comfort, but he knew it was no substitute for the protection his guards would provide.

With little urging, he nudged his horse forward down the rocky path. They maintained a slow, steady pace, as the uneven ground could be treacherous to traverse. The sun was beating high overhead when they finally reached the deep cool shadows at the edge of the forest. His unease grew slightly as he approached the tree line. The shadows of the trees seemed deeper than they should be, the rustling leaves just a touch too loud. He dismissed the feeling as mere fancy, but as his eyes drifted over the darkened path ahead, the unease lingered in the back of his mind, like a whisper of something yet to come.

Prince Coriander looped the reins casually over a tree branch once he dismounted, leaving the horse plenty of slack to wander and graze. Zedd was well-trained and would not pull free from the loose tether unless in distress. He removed some of the tack and stacked it neatly on the ground nearby. He brushed down the horse, cooing softly as he did so, the rhythmic motion of the brush calming his nerves. "You're the only one who truly listens, aren't you, Zedd?" he murmured, a faint smile on his lips. The horse neighed softly in appreciation, nudging Coriander's hand as if in agreement. Coriander chuckled, but there was a sadness in it. He often spoke to Zedd this way, sharing thoughts he couldn't voice to anyone else. The horse wouldn't judge him, and wouldn't expect him to have all the answers. "If only people were as easy to understand as you," he whispered, scratching Zedd's head fondly. The horse's warmth against his hand was a rare comfort.

    He removed several stowed items from the saddlebags, each piece a small reminder of home—his mother's quilt, painstakingly stitched with patterns of the royal crest; the bottle of wine, a gift from his father on his last birthday; the cheese and dried meat, wrapped carefully by the castle's cook, who always slipped him an extra portion as if he were still a boy. Coriander spread the quilt out on the grass, feeling a pang of longing for the simplicity of the castle kitchen, where the weight of his future didn't seem so heavy. He laid a bottle of wine and an unwrapped cloth of cheese and dried meat on it. As he stripped off his sweat-dampened tunic, revealing his full physique, he couldn't help but feel a pang of discomfort. He laid out the tunic to dry, followed by his trousers, and laid upon the quilt in his loincloth.

Despite the cooling nights of the approaching autumn, the days were still warm; a lingering echo of summer that Coriander was determined to savor. This was the best way to enjoy the sun, far away from the prying eyes and endless demands that came with being the crown prince. Here, he could forget for a moment who he was supposed to be—just a young man lying in the sun, free from titles and responsibilities. Yet even in this solitude, a part of him couldn't fully escape the sense of duty that always hovered just at the edge of his thoughts, like a shadow cast by the sun itself.

The wine was sweet, with a cool burn as he drank. The meat was tender, though a bit bland, but paired well with the cheese. He ate and drank his fill, then laid back casually upon the quilt, his hands resting behind his head as he stared up at the clear blue sky. A gentle breeze rustled through the leaves, and the calm sounds of the forest tickled at Coriander's ears. But beneath the tranquility, he couldn't shake a faint unease—a sense that the forest was watching him, waiting. As his eyes drifted closed, the unease continued to linger in the back of his mind. Before he knew it, sleep overtook him.

Chapter Two

Coriander's eyes snapped open. Something was amiss.

The sky above had begun to deepen into purple, with the last vestiges of orange light coloring the western horizon. A few early stars dotted the east, and the air had grown crisp and chilly. Nearby, Zedd neighed softly, calmly grazing on a patch of scruffy grass. This at least put Coriander's mind somewhat at ease; if there were any immediate danger, Zedd would have certainly alerted him. Still, a knot of unease twisted in his gut.

He sat up slowly, straining his ears to catch the sound that had disturbed his sleep. It took a few minutes, but there it was: a distant splashing sound coming from the woods. He quickly slipped on his boots, leaving them loosely laced, and grabbed the sheathed sword from the pile of equipment.

The forest was not overly dense, making passage relatively easy. Thanks to his years of hunting, he moved swiftly and silently, carefully avoiding brambles that could scratch his exposed skin. Before long, he located a deer path leading in the same direction, aiding his travel. Again, he heard splashing up ahead, closer now.

The deer path came to an abrupt end, opening up into a clearing dimly lit by the last orange rays of the setting sun. A small stream trickled over a large crop of rocks, tumbling gently down as a small, quiet waterfall into a pond below. The edge of the water was lined with reeds, and small dragonflies darted about.

Despite the tranquil scene, something felt off. He saw nothing to explain the splashing he had heard. No person or animal seemed to be in the vicinity, and the dark water of the pond was smooth, save for the ripples caused by the waterfall.

Suddenly, a figure burst out of the pond, gasping sharply as he surfaced, water cascading off his body. Coriander quickly ducked behind a cluster of bushes at the clearing's edge, watching intently as the man swam to shore. The stranger had bright red hair spilling wetly down his shoulders and back, and a toned but slender frame. His skin was pale and lightly freckled, the contrast evident even in the fading light.

With his body fully on display, Coriander's eyes instinctively roved over him, taking in every detail. The man was shapely, thin but muscle-toned, and his light patch of red hair instantly drew Coriander's gaze to his long manhood. The prince let out a quiet, involuntary gasp, heat pooling in his loins as he marveled at the man's flawless form. Never before had he seen such a sight stir such deep desire within him.

As if sensing he was being watched, the stranger's sparkling green eyes suddenly scanned the forest around him. Coriander held his breath, but the man's eyes locked onto the bushes where he was concealed. Without a word, the man sprinted away.

"No! Wait!" Coriander called out, stumbling from his hiding place, desperation lacing his voice. Dropping his sword, he gave chase, the man disappearing into the dense woods, his passage marked only by the faintest rustling of leaves. Coriander burst through the same bushes, the brambles tearing at his skin with hot, sharp pain. But the man had vanished into the forest's shadows, leaving only the sound of Coriander's ragged breaths in the quiet night.

The prince made it back to the castle late at night, moving quietly through the dimly lit corridors. The flickering torchlight cast long shadows on the stone walls as he carefully ascended the stairs, each step echoing faintly in the silence. Not a single guard or member of the staff crossed his path—a small blessing, as he had no desire to explain his late-night excursion to his father. Though he had recently celebrated his 19th birthday, his father remained as overbearing and protective as ever, always fearing for the safety of his only son, the heir to the throne. But that understanding did little to soothe the frustration gnawing at Coriander, a frustration born of the desire for freedom and the burdens of responsibility.

Reaching his room, Coriander slipped inside, the door closing softly behind him. He collapsed onto his bed, half-tangled in the fur blankets, unable to sleep. The shutters were open, letting the cool night breeze wash over the room as pale moonlight played across the stone floor. But the serenity of the night did nothing to calm the turmoil in his mind.

No matter how hard he tried, he couldn't shake the image of the man from the forest. The scene replayed endlessly in his mind— the stranger's striking red hair, his pale freckled skin, the way he had moved so gracefully from the water. What sort of spell had the stranger cast over him? Sure, he had often admired the male form before. There was no shortage of well-built men around the castle—guards, trainers, men he had sparred with countless times. But none had ever stirred such a deep, confusing desire within him.

He sighed, turning onto his back as the scene from the woods played out once more in his mind, while the first morning birds began to chirp outside. Dawn was fast approaching, and he had yet to sleep. As the stranger crossed his mind again, Coriander became acutely aware of his growing desire beneath the blankets. He groaned softly, reaching down to adjust himself, but the feeling only intensified, a need that he knew he would have to address himself.

His mind drifted back to the dusk-lit grotto as his hand began to move slowly. He could almost feel the cool water trickling down the stranger's chest, his bright red hair clinging to his shoulders. Coriander's breathing quickened, his hand moving with growing urgency. In his mind's eye, he watched the stranger climb out of the pond, water streaming down his pale body, his green eyes glimmering with mischief. The happy little trail of fire-red hair leading to his erect cock.

As if drawn by an invisible force, Coriander imagined stepping toward him, their gazes locked across the meadow. The man smiled, beckoning him closer, and Coriander felt his heart race, his own manhood straining beneath his loincloth. He released his erect member. It throbbed with need as his hand took a firm grip, and began stroking it.

The distance between them vanished, and the stranger's hands found his body, warm and firm, pulling him into an embrace that sent shivers down his spine. The prince could almost feel the man's heat against his skin, the pressure of his excitement mirroring his own.

Coriander's breathing grew ragged, his hand moving faster, the tension in his body building to an unbearable peak. In his mind, he bent slowly toward the stranger, their lips brushing together in a tentative kiss...

The door to his room suddenly creaked open, just as Coriander spilled his seed across his stomach with a muffled groan. He scrambled to cover himself with the blankets, his heart pounding in his chest. The young chamberlain who had entered froze, his eyes widening before quickly dropping to the floor. Coriander recognized him—Samuel, a boy barely a year younger than the prince himself, who had only recently begun his service in the royal quarters.

"My apologies, sire..." Samuel stammered, his voice trembling, but Coriander cut him off sharply.

"Get out!" the prince commanded, his voice rough with embarrassment as he clutched the blankets around himself.

Samuel nodded quickly, his face flushed as he hurriedly backed out of the room, murmuring apologies as he closed the door behind him. Coriander let out a long, frustrated sigh, lifting the now sticky blanket off his stomach. The fire in his loins had finally been sated, but the encounter left him feeling more confused than ever. He groaned, running a hand through his tousled hair, his mind still reeling from the intensity of his fantasy.

Rising from the bed, he gathered what he needed for a bath, hoping the water would wash away the remnants of his desire—and the troubling thoughts that had accompanied it. As he moved toward the washroom, his mind lingered on the memory of the stranger, and he couldn't help but wonder what kind of spell had truly been cast over him that night in the woods.

Chapter Three

It was nearly two weeks before Coriander could return to the grotto. His days were consumed by lessons, meetings, and training, leaving him no time to escape to the woods. But now, with a free weekend ahead, he finally had a chance. He had carefully laid the groundwork with his father, claiming he planned a hunting trip that would take him away from the kingdom for a few days.

Despite his protests, his father insisted on sending an escort with him. Coriander had just finished packing Zedd with camping gear when a voice called his name across the courtyard. He turned to see his friend Leon approaching.

Dark-haired and nearly a full hand taller than Coriander, the roguish young man was a welcome sight. Leon had lost his left eye in an accident as a child and wore a patch to cover it. This only seemed to enhance his good looks, and he rarely spent a night alone.

"Guess who got stuck on escort duty to babysit some spoiled noble brat?" Leon teased as he approached. Coriander clasped arms with his friend in greeting. Leon was the son of a high noble, so they had been friends since practically the nursery. Leon had chosen to serve with the military and was well on his way to moving up the ranks.

"At least you don't have to be followed around by some high and mighty soldier-wanna-be," Coriander replied with a laugh, giving his friend a playful shove. "Two whole nights without a woman to keep you warm. How will you ever survive?"

"Guess I'll have to cozy up to you at the campfire," Leon retorted, looking him up and down. "You're certainly not the worst lady of the evening I've spent time with."

A heat crept up Coriander's neck, a mix of embarrassment and something he couldn't quite name. His mind wandered unbidden to that night in the woods. Leon though? He had never considered it before.

"Yeah, well, I expect the coin up front," the prince shot back, drawing a laugh from his friend.

They led Zedd across the courtyard to the gate where Leon's mare, Gemstone, awaited. The horse was stark white, save for a diamond-shaped patch of black on its chest. It was a stark contrast to the rusty brown of Zedd. Gemstone neighed in greeting as they approached, and Zedd took the opportunity to nuzzle the familiar mare.

"Even your horse gets more action than you do, Cory," Leon teased as he climbed into his horse's saddle.

"Shut it, Leon," Coriander growled in mock malice. "Or there's going to be an unpleasant hunting accident this weekend." He pulled himself up into Zedd's saddle. Leon laughed again, and this time Coriander joined him. They rode off through the gate together.

"So, what's this really about?" Leon asked after a while. They had ridden pretty far, and evening was fast approaching. They were still an hour or two from the woods.

"What do you mean?" Coriander asked innocently, though his heart began to race. Leon gave him a long, knowing stare.

"You HATE hunting!" his friend exclaimed. "So, you must be up to something else."

Coriander busied himself with Zedd's reins, avoiding Leon's gaze as guilt gnawed at him. "It's a girl, isn't it?" Leon asked suddenly. Coriander startled in his saddle, his mind scrambling for an answer as Leon chuckled, sensing victory. "Some young farm girl caught your eye? Someone daddy would never approve of you being with? Sounds about right?"

"Yeah," Coriander lied after a moment, "sounds about right."

"Ha! I knew it!" His friend cheered. "What's she like?"

Coriander's thoughts drifted back to the evening in the woods, the image of the red-haired stranger rising from the water burning in his mind. He felt himself stiffening at the memory. "Long red hair," he replied, his voice lower. "Rosy light skin, spattered with freckles. Gorgeous green eyes, seeming to alight from within."

"Well endowed?" Leon asked, grinning as he held his hands up to his chest as if gripping a pair of melons.

Coriander's thoughts flashed to that night. The fiery red hair had perfectly outlined the stranger's impressive manhood. His cheeks flushed, and he felt himself grow even harder. "Very well endowed," he coughed out in confirmation.

"Then I approve!" Leon exclaimed, batting his friend on the shoulder as they trotted next to each other. "You're taking steps to prevent her from bearing a child, right? Your father would lose it if she bore an illegitimate heir."

Coriander almost choked at the question, barely stopping himself from laughing at the absurdity of it. "That won't be a problem," he assured. "I'll be careful."

They rode in silence for a short time, the last village fading into the distance as the dense forest loomed ahead, the shadows growing longer. Coriander's mind raced as he thought about how to explain his need to wander off alone once they reached the woods. He realized Leon was no longer beside him and turned to see his friend had stopped.

"There's a tavern back there," Leon explained. "I'm going to grab a couple pints." He tossed something to Coriander—a guard's signal whistle. "If I camp up on those cliffs, will it be close enough to hear the whistle if you're in trouble?"

Coriander considered the distance and realized what his friend was offering him. "Yes," he replied, his voice full of gratitude.

Leon waved it off, a teasing smile on his face. "So help me, Coriander, if you get yourself hurt out there, I'll kill you myself."

The prince laughed, and they traded grips before parting ways. Coriander watched as Leon rode off toward the tavern, the weight of his friend's understanding and unspoken trust settling over him. He turned Zedd toward the forest, the anticipation building in his chest.

Chapter Four

Before setting up camp, Coriander left Zedd tethered to a sturdy tree branch and checked the grotto. The place was deserted, devoid of any recent signs of visitors. Disappointed but not disheartened, he returned to his camp spot and began setting up. By the time the light had faded, his small tent was up, and a fire pit lined with stones was ready for use.

As night fell, a fire roared in the pit, and Zedd was fully unbridled, save for his lead. The horse received a grateful brushing and a juicy apple as a reward for his patience.

Coriander sat by the fire, poking at the embers with a stick. He considered heating some meat, but his appetite had deserted him. Instead, he opened a bottle of wine and sipped it slowly, staring into the flames. What if the stranger never returned? The thought gnawed at him, each flicker of the fire taunting him with the possibility that his yearning might remain unfulfilled. He finished the bottle, tilting it back to extract the last drop before tossing it into his rubbish sack. He thought about opening another bottle but decided against it, feeling tipsy from the first.

He lay back on his bedroll, staring up at the twinkling stars. His mind drifted back to that night in the woods, stirring his passion. He absentmindedly adjusted the tightness of his loincloth, his member pulsing with anticipation. The vivid image of the stranger, with his fiery red hair cascading over his sculpted body, persisted in his thoughts. The vision of the stranger's muscular frame and inviting red bush made him rub at the bulge in his trousers again, his arousal intensifying.

Realizing he was getting carried away, Coriander sighed and turned onto his stomach. The pressure against the bedroll and the hard ground beneath was uncomfortable, but he ignored it and closed his eyes. Eventually, sleep took him.

In his dream, the red-haired stranger emerged from the water, glistening under the dappled sunlight. He seemed to walk on water as he stepped out of the pond, his movements graceful and confident.

Coriander's breath caught at the sight. The man pulled his wet hair into a ponytail, his dimples accentuating as he turned to face Coriander. The stranger's bright red bush seemed to call out to him, displaying exactly what he desired.

The man's erection stood firm, water dripping from its tip and forming a small puddle at his feet. Its size and girth had increased, veins protruding along its length, drawing Coriander's gaze.

"Coriander," the stranger whispered in a husky voice, extending a hand toward him. Coriander took a step forward, but the world around him blurred. He tried to close the distance, but the stranger remained frustratingly out of reach. Desperation fueled his run, the colors of the world swirling chaotically around him.

"Find me," the man's final whisper echoed softly.

Coriander woke abruptly, turning to one side as the last remnants of the wine forced their way up. He breathed heavily, waiting for his stomach to settle. The early morning was cold, the fire from the night reduced to smoldering ashes. Dew glistened on the grass in the pale morning light. His shirt clung damply to his body, and he shivered as he poked the ashes with a stick. A few embers glowed faintly, and with some tinder and small sticks, he managed to rekindle the flames.

He stripped off his damp clothes, arranging them by the fire to dry. After dressing in a fresh set from his pack, he took a sip from his water skin. His stomach protested but settled as he drank.

Coriander ventured into the woods to set up snares, munching on day-old bread as he went. His stomach grumbled but held firm this time. By the time the snares were set, he felt like himself again.

He wandered back to the grotto, finding it still empty. Midday approached, bringing warmth to the air. Golden rays of sunlight filtered through the trees, reflecting off the clear blue water of the pond. The small waterfall's gentle melody played on, while fish swam gracefully below.

Not even big enough to eat, Coriander mused with a small laugh. The pond looked inviting. Stripping off his clothes and loincloth, he left them on a dry rock. *Who would see him?*

He stepped into the water, feeling the chill of the mud at the bottom. Though cold, it was refreshing against the warm day. He took a deep breath and dove in. The cold water shocked him but felt invigorating. He surfaced, gasping for air, and floated on his back, letting the sun warm his skin. His blond curls, tamed by the water, floated around his head like a golden halo.

The forest was alive with nature's sounds—songbirds flitting among the trees, dragonflies buzzing, and a bullfrog croaking nearby. Coriander sighed, feeling the whole plan might be a bust. He climbed out of the pond through the gap in the reeds that the stranger had used. Gathering his clothes, he slipped on his boots and headed back down the deer path to camp.

Chapter Five

Coriander lay on a blanket spread out in the bright sunlight, still stark naked. He had dried off long ago, and his hair had returned to its natural curliness. The warmth of the sun felt wonderful against his skin.

He was drifting in and out of sleep when he suddenly heard the sound of hooves approaching. Panicking, he quickly flipped one corner of the blanket to cover himself as a white horse crested the nearest ridge. The black diamond on its chest was unmistakable. Coriander sighed; this was the last thing he needed.

"Cory!" Leon called out as soon as he spotted him. He slowed Gemstone to a trot as he approached. Leon took in the scene with a raised eyebrow. "I'm not interrupting something, am I?" he asked, his tone serious.

"No, not at all," Coriander murmured, his voice tinged with embarrassment.

"Stood up?" Leon asked sympathetically. Then he brightened. "Good thing I came along!"

"That remains to be seen," Coriander replied with a mock growl. Leon laughed heartily.

"You remember that knife Duke What's-His-Face gave me a few years ago? The one with the pearl inlay?"

Coriander scratched his head, then nodded. "Well," Leon continued with a smug grin, "I traded it for a jug of old man Parker's legendary apple shine!" He held up the corked jug triumphantly.

Coriander rolled his eyes, though he felt a surge of excitement despite his earlier discomfort. Old man Parker's apple shine was famous, and hard to come by. Even if the apple variety was standard, it was still a treat.

Coriander got to his feet, carefully wrapping the blanket around himself to maintain some modesty. He marched back to camp, doing his best to avoid exposing himself further.

"What were you doing anyway?" Leon asked curiously as Gemstone trotted beside Coriander.

"Just a little sunbathing," Coriander replied tersely.

"Evening out those tan lines, huh?" Leon teased with a grin. Coriander shot him a look. "Alright, alright, touchy subject."

Back at camp, Zedd whinnied a greeting to Gemstone. Leon tossed her rein over a nearby branch so the two horses could nuzzle each other. Coriander directed Leon to the snares he had set up and asked him to check them while he got dressed, emphasizing that he wasn't drinking any of the shine on an empty stomach.

Both Leon and Coriander's stomachs agreed with this sentiment, and Leon disappeared into the woods.

Coriander dressed and set up camp. He stoked the fire and hung a small pot over the flames on a portable iron hook. He filled it with water and began chopping fresh vegetables. As the stew bubbled, the aroma of simmering vegetables and seasoning filled the air, mingling with the earthy scent of the campfire smoke. After adding the vegetables and seasoning cubes, the stew began to smell delicious by the time Leon returned.

Leon carried a sizable hare over his shoulder, but the other snare had been empty. Still, one hare was ample for the stew. Coriander worked on skinning and trimming it while Leon unpacked and brushed down Gemstone.

"Not gonna lie," Leon said casually as he packed the grooming brush back into his saddlebag, "I got a little turned around in there. Never been great with the woods. But I found this awesome hidden pond!"

Coriander froze, his knife pausing in its task of chopping the hare meat. Had Leon stumbled upon the same pond? Was his secret exposed? Panic set in, mingling with a sense of dread.

"Looked like a great spot to swim," Leon continued. "But it's probably too chilly this time of year. Are you going to stare at that meat all night, or are you going to put it in?"

Coriander snapped back to the present, startled by the sudden question. He looked up to find Leon standing close, their knees nearly touching. Coriander's gaze lingered for a moment on his friend's crotch, sparking an unexpected flutter in his chest. He quickly met Leon's dark eyes.

"Seriously, I'm starving, Cory. Hurry up," Leon said, giving Coriander's thigh a playful nudge.

Coriander laughed and scraped the meat off the cutting board into the stew. It wouldn't take long to cook. Leon sat down beside him on the bedroll, their knees pressed together. Coriander tried to ignore the warmth of the contact as Leon set down two clay mugs and popped the cork on the apple shine. The sweet aroma filled the air, tempting him despite his stomach's protests.

"Not until I've eaten," Coriander protested, crossing his arms over his midsection.

"One cup while the stew cooks won't kill you," Leon replied, pouring two small glasses. Coriander sighed, lifted his cup, and clinked it against Leon's. He took a sip, the familiar warmth of the apple shine soothing his senses.

Chapter Six

The campfire's embers cast a dim, warm glow across the darkened clearing, the surrounding trees casting long shadows as the night deepened. The stew was long gone, its pot capsized on the ground nearby. Raucous laughter filled the camp.

"Swear to it," Leon interrupted, trying to cross his fingers and somehow failing spectacularly. He stared at his hand for a moment as if in great betrayal, then laughed and returned to the story. "I only had a few seconds to make a decision. So I dove into the latrine. It was that or get married." Coriander roared with laughter. "Literally the shittiest day of my life."

As the fire's glow flickered, Coriander's laughter and hiccups filled the night air, masking the undercurrent of a more serious conversation that was about to unfold. His laugh was interrupted by a hiccup, followed by a loud and long belch. Both men began roaring with laughter again. The prince swayed slightly, decided not to fight it, and laid back in the cool grass along the edge of the bedroll. A moment later, Leon toppled over and joined him, his head resting against Coriander's shoulder.

"You really have a way with women, don't you?" Coriander slurred, his words thick with the effects of the appleshine.

"I don't mean to be," Leon replied, his words also slurred but carrying a tone of seriousness. "I just haven't found the perfect one yet."

"Not from lack of trying!" Coriander shot back, laughing and completely oblivious to the tone of his friend's voice.

"Yeah," Leon sighed. "I want someone I know I can spend forever with. Someone who can be like a best friend, and I can love wholeheartedly."

Coriander tried to raise his head slightly, succeeded somewhat, and stared at the dark mess of hair atop his friend's head. Finally he had caught on to the sudden change of tone.

"She's out there," he reassured.

"Yeah." Leon replied, unconvincingly.

Time seemed to freeze for Coriander as Leon's words sank in, each beat of his heart echoing louder in the tense silence that followed.

"I see the way you stare at me sometimes, even if you don't realize you're doing it."
Coriander's breath quickened. His mind raced as the weight of Leon's words hit him. "It's okay," Leon

assured, rising up on one elbow so he could look Coriander in the eye. "I'm not offended. In fact, I see it as a bit endearing." He laid his head back down, but now it was on top of Coriander's shoulder. He moved a little closer, and put one arm around the prince's midsection. "You forget Cory, I've known you your entire life. You've never really been interested in women. You've courted a few only to keep your father off your back, but that's never where your heart has been."

Coriander could feel the warmth of Leon's body pressed against him, intensified by the appleshine coursing through his veins. He could even smell the sweet scent of it on Leon's breath as he spoke. Despite his best efforts, he could feel his loins beginning to respond. Leon lifted himself back up, pulling himself even closer and tighter against his friend.

"All I'm saying," he whispered, "is that I'm open to it." Leon leaned even closer, his hand sliding up Coriander's chest. He was so close now, the prince could feel his warm, sweet breath against his cheek. Their noses brushed together, but suddenly all Coriander could think about was flowing red hair. He abruptly pushed Leon back.

"You're drunk, this isn't right," the prince stated with finality. Leon sat up away from his friend, his eye glassy with unshed tears and his expression crumpled with a mix of vulnerability and hurt. "We should get some sleep and discuss this in the morning."

Leon nodded quietly as Coriander stood. The prince helped his friend settle onto the bedroll, the gentle rustle of the blanket the only sound as he tucked it in carefully, his thoughts churning. Leon was asleep before he had even finished tucking him in.

Coriander stumbled to the tent, struggled with the catch on the flap for a moment, and crawled inside. Leon had claimed the only bedroll, so Coriander made do with a folded blanket, spreading it out as best as he could for a semblance of comfort. He too fell asleep quickly, barely having time to lay his head down.

Chapter Seven

Morning came far too soon as Coriander awoke to a throbbing headache. He groaned, the dull pain pulsing behind his eyes as he tried to sit up, only to have the world spin around him. It wasn't just his head that ached, though; another part of him was uncomfortably alert. He groaned again, this time in exasperation.

"Would you knock it off," he muttered disgustedly to his own saluting member. Then a thought crossed his mind: why was he naked? He didn't remember undressing. But he must have undressed at some point in the night, as his clothes lay crumpled next to his makeshift bed. The appleshine burning inside him must have made him too hot during the night, leading him to strip them off.

"Leon," he groaned, finally sitting up. His memories of the night were spotty at best, but he still remembered how close their lips had been, and the look of hurt in his friend's eyes. A pang of guilt twisted in his chest. What had he been thinking? He struggled to slip on his trousers, tying the strings tightly over his insistent arousal, hoping it would take the hint. He crawled to the tent entrance and undid the partially open flap.

The camp beyond was empty. His bedroll was still spread out on the ground before the freshly built-up fire, the blanket folded and placed neatly on top. Zedd whinnied a greeting from nearby, but Gemstone was no longer tethered next to him.

Coriander sighed with regret. He wondered how much Leon remembered. After all, his friend had drunk far more of the 'shine than he had, and his own memory was still fuzzy.

The soup pot from the night before had been cleaned and now stood on the edge of the embers, filled with water. It was close enough to the fire to warm up, but not to boil. Outside, on the rocks next to it, stood one of the clay cups, with a piece of paper and cloth sticking out of it. Coriander picked it up, unfolding the paper first.

"*Cory,*" it read in Leon's flowing script, "*Hopefully she's just running late. I'll be in my camp on the cliffs if you need anything. We return in the morning. —Leon.*"

He folded the note and placed it gently beside the cup. The morning air was crisp, yet the weight of the night still lingered, heavy and confusing. Leon's absence left a hollow feeling in the camp, one that the warming fire couldn't chase away.

Leon had also left a small packet containing a mint tea blend. He poured the steaming water into the cup with the cloth packet and gave it a swirl. The smell of mint began to permeate the camp. Coriander sighed, just as a rough voice shattered the peace.

"Hey, 'old it right there," a man's rough voice rasped out. Zedd whinnied a loud warning—too late. Coriander dropped the clay cup, and it shattered on the rocks below. "Turn around real slow, and tell your beast to calm down before it gets a bolt to the chest."

Coriander did as instructed, cooing softly to Zedd until the bucking horse began to calm. He faced the man, standing just slightly back in the brush of the woods. He had approached from downwind and had to have been damn silent to sneak up on Zedd. The man wore worn black leathers and had a scar running down one cheek. Most importantly, he had a crossbow leveled at the prince's chest.

"Which of those bags has the coin?" the bandit asked calmly.

"I don't have any coin with me," Coriander stuttered. His gaze fell on his sword, lying against his pack. No good though; it was between him and the bandit. He'd never reach it before the man pulled the trigger, and at this range, he was unlikely to miss.

"Don't lie to me, noble. Which bag?"

"Why do you think I'm a noble?" Coriander asked, his tone laced with a forced calm, though his gaze betrayed the calculation as it flickered to his sword. The bandit gestured to the pile of equipment with the tip of his crossbow.

"Them saddle bags there have the royal crest stamped into them. You're either a noble or a thief yourself. Either way, if you want to live today, you'll give up the coin."

Coriander's mind raced. He could see the twitch in the bandit's trigger finger, the way his eyes darted to the sword. The man was nervous, desperate. Desperation made people dangerous. Coriander's heart pounded in his chest, each beat echoing the seconds ticking away, each breath a reminder of how close death stood. It was true—he'd brought no coins with him. But he did have a few things one would consider valuable. Maybe he could offer them to the bandit instead. He was about to say as much when the robber let out a sudden high-pitched squeal. The crossbow fell to the ground, its bolt firing off harmlessly into the tent.

The man seemed to wriggle in place, his body contorting unnaturally as if it couldn't decide which way to move. The air around them seemed to hum with an unnatural energy. Coriander could feel it on his skin, like static before a storm. The man's eyes widened in horror as his body twisted and shrank, the scent of earth and fur filling the air. The sound of bones shifting was soft but unmistakable, sending a shiver down Coriander's spine. His face elongated, nose twitching and sprouting whiskers. His ears slid up to the top of his head, stretching and growing fur in a disconcerting metamorphosis. With each twist, he shrank further into himself until all that remained was a pile of trembling clothing.

After a moment, the pile of clothing moved as a gray bunny struggled out from underneath it. Its ears and nose twitched in every direction, and its eyes filled with terror. It took off, darting into the woods right past...

A flash of red hair.

Coriander's breath caught sharply. There before him, standing right behind where the bandit had stood, was the red-haired stranger. The same man—no, not a man at all, something else entirely—who had haunted his thoughts. He was just as naked as before, yet the way the light danced off his skin, how the foliage framed his figure, was otherworldly. Everything about this encounter screamed of something beyond the ordinary.

They stared at each other for what seemed like an eternity as Zedd neighed softly nearby. At least Zedd wasn't bothered by the stranger's presence. The same couldn't be said for Coriander, whose cheeks burned as his trousers tightened again.

"Are you some kind of witch?" Coriander called out softly, trying not to sound accusatory. The stranger's bright hair shook back and forth as he denied it.

"Not exactly." His voice was masculine but soft and sweet.

"What did you do to him?" Coriander nodded in the direction the rabbit had run.

"It'll wear off in a few hours, he'll be fine. Assuming he isn't eaten by a fox between now and then." The stranger smiled warmly, as if enjoying his own joke. Coriander took a step forward, and the stranger turned as if to flee.

"Wait!" the prince called. The stranger stopped, his head turning enough to expose one ear. It wasn't rounded but came to a point at the top. He hadn't noticed before, as they'd always been hidden underneath his hair. "When can I see you again?"

"You won't," the man replied sternly. With a flurry of wind, gossamer wings unfurled from the stranger's back, shimmering like morning dew caught in the sunlight. They fluttered delicately, yet with a power that stirred the air around them, lifting the stranger from the ground. Coriander watched in awe as the man's form blurred and shrank, like a dandelion puff caught on a breeze, until he was no more than a flicker of light darting through the trees.

    Coriander stood rooted to the spot, his breath caught in his throat. The forest seemed to hold its breath with him, as if the world itself couldn't believe what had just happened. His mind raced, trying to reconcile the impossible with reality. He'd heard the stories as a child, tales of trickster spirits and ancient magic, but to see one—to speak to one... His heart pounded, the exhilaration mingling with a fear that he couldn't quite name. He wanted to laugh, to cry, to chase after the fleeting figure that had vanished into the woods, leaving only questions in its wake.

    The stranger was a fairy.

Chapter Eight

He and Leon had ridden back to the castle in near silence. Awkwardness burned in the air between them, but neither seemed ready to talk about it. Coriander certainly didn't bring up the near miss with the bandit. Awkwardness or not, Leon would never let him wander off alone again.

They parted ways as soon as they passed through the gates, and Coriander watched his friend ride off, unsure of what he could do to fix the situation. He had always cared for Leon, but despite Leon's claim otherwise, he had never thought of him as anything other than a friend.

His princely duties took over again, and he fell into the grindstone of everyday life. But that didn't deter him, as he'd found a new purpose. Any spare moment he had now was spent in the library, reading all the accounts he could find about fairy-folk—every account, every tale, every children's story.

The information varied wildly, claiming a variety of powers, dark magic, misfortune, even sudden death at their mere sight. Some claimed iron could kill them, others said it weakened them and made it possible to trap them. Other stories touched on their eating habits, everything from newborn babies to simple dishes of milk and honey.

Only a few sources seemed to agree on anything, and those few nuggets of knowledge were where Coriander began to build his understanding.

As the days passed, Coriander found himself increasingly distracted during courtly functions, his thoughts returning again and again to the stranger with the red hair and green eyes. Despite his busy schedule, the obsession threatened to consume him.

Coriander saw little of Leon over the next few days, the knight seeming to avoid him. This also weighed heavily on the Prince's mind. He had hurt his friend with his rejection, and it only added to Coriander's anxiety. What could he have done differently? Truly, he had never considered his friend in that way, never believing Leon would even be interested in such things. The knight was a notorious lady's man. Coming from any other source, he wouldn't even have believed it. But Leon had tried to kiss him, something he surely hadn't imagined.

Now, on top of it all, the King—his father—was parading him in front of prospective future wives. Several noble daughters from surrounding lands had been invited to the kingdom for a party. Coriander was expected to host each of these guests while his father negotiated with their parents. Whoever provided the most profitable dowry would secure the right to marry Coriander, and thus their daughter's future position as Queen.

It was another thing weighing on the Prince's mind. The entire marriage process was abhorrent to Coriander, but it was the tradition the kingdom had upheld for generations.

A tradition he would abolish once he was king, Coriander thought gravely. He snapped out of his dark thoughts long enough to give Lady Miranda a forced smile as he took her hand. The daughter of a high noble, Coriander had a feeling she was the most likely candidate for his father to choose. Her parents came from a hugely successful land baron, who alone would greatly increase the size of the kingdom should he offer his lands in the dowry.

The soft glow of the chandeliers bathed the ballroom in a golden light, casting flickering shadows on the polished marble floor. The band struck up a slow and romantic waltz. Coriander followed along easily, the dance being one he had practiced many times throughout his youth. His eyes wandered the room, passing over the casually dressed knights standing at attention. Leon was not among them, which worried the prince more than anything else. This was definitely not the sort of function his friend would ever miss, knowing the high potential of being able to bed one of the Ladies for the night.

Leon's absence was glaring. Normally, he would have been at Coriander's side, making snide remarks about the court's politics, or flirting with the ladies to pass the time. But now, his silence was heavy, like a storm cloud hovering just out of sight. Coriander sighed to himself, the distraction to his thoughts causing him to misstep in the dance and nearly trip over the young lady hanging off his arm.

"Sorry," he muttered a half-hearted apology.

"It's no trouble," she whispered back, using the distraction to seductively slide one hand across his back, giving his butt a quick squeeze. She gave him a flirtatious smile, which Coriander promptly ignored.

Much of the night from that point repeated itself, only with the Prince leading a different Lady on his arm for each subsequent dance. Each Lady's touch was feather-light yet demanding, and Coriander could feel the weight of their gazes on him as they moved together. But no matter how well they danced, or how charming their smiles, his thoughts kept drifting back to the stranger with the impossibly green eyes.

As Coriander danced with each Lady, he couldn't shake the feeling that something was wrong—like a storm brewing on the horizon. The stranger's words haunted him, a riddle he couldn't solve. And then there was Leon, whose absence was more telling than any words. Something was changing, and Coriander wasn't sure he was ready for it.

Finally, the night began to wind down, and Coriander was able to excuse himself for the night and return to his room. The stranger, Leon, and now the noble Ladies—it was all too much. He had always valued Leon's friendship above all else, but now, with this new tension between them, Coriander wasn't sure what he felt. The stranger had ignited something in him—something wild and untamed—that he couldn't ignore, even if it meant hurting Leon.

Coriander stared at the ceiling, his thoughts a tangled mess of duty, desire, and doubt. The stranger's face loomed in his mind, vivid and consuming. But behind it lingered Leon's hurt expression, the weight of his father's expectations, and the suffocating reality of the path laid out before him. As sleep claimed him,

Coriander couldn't shake the feeling that whatever choice he made, it would change everything.

All his energy gone, he barely managed to finish stripping before he was under the warm wool blankets, the stress of the day bleeding into much-needed sleep.

Coriander took the stranger's hand as the band started playing an intimate slow song. Their bodies pressed together, hand in hand, as they began to waltz in time to the music. Coriander could feel the warmth of the stranger's body against his own and realized far too late they were both stark naked.

The prince glanced around the room in embarrassment, taking note of the knights in their fine clothes. Each stood at attention, their eyes staring off into the distance as decorum dictated. The waltz played on, but the notes were strangely muted, as if coming from a great distance. The room felt both too vast and too small, the walls closing in as the knights and nobles faded into the shadows. Only the stranger's touch remained real, warm and insistent, pulling Coriander deeper into the embrace of the dream.

Coriander's eyes met his father's, sitting on the high-backed chair along one wall, below the banner carrying the kingdom's crest. His father seemed impatient, staring at him intently and tapping one foot.

"Do not take too long to choose, my son; there are many options," his father shouted out to him across the ballroom floor. Coriander blushed, turning from his father's gaze and instead falling on his best friend. Leon stood nearby, also nude like the stranger, looking as impatient as the king.

"Hurry up, Cory," he said. "It's my turn next unless you're going to ignore me again."

Coriander turned toward his friend, about to answer. However, a strong grip held him tight. The stranger pulled him back close, beautiful gossamer wings springing from his back.
"Listen not to them," the stranger said with sweet words, "for only I can satisfy you." He pulled the prince close, their lips pressing together in a soft, passionate kiss. They parted with a soft moan, the stranger holding Coriander's gaze with his impossibly green eyes.

The ballroom stretched and contracted, its walls breathing like a living thing. The music slowed, each note a heavy echo that reverberated through his bones. Faces in the crowd blurred, indistinct shadows that flickered like candle flames. And then, the stranger—impossibly close, his breath warm against Coriander's ear, whispering words that were both a promise and a threat.

"Find me, my prince."

Chapter Nine

Coriander woke in a cold sweat. Cool night air filtered into the room from the partially open shutters, finally beginning to overpower the dying fire in the fireplace. A couple of the remaining embers popped in futile protest.

Tossing the blanket from himself with a sigh, the prince crossed the room. However, the small rack next to the fireplace was devoid of any firewood. Coriander shivered, the sweat on his nude body made even colder by the night air.

He made his way back to the bedside, stopping briefly to grab the wool blanket from the bed and wrap himself in it. A quick tug on the rope above his nightstand would bring a chamberlain to his room in haste.

Waiting by the fireplace to help stay warm, it was only a few minutes before the latch on his door opened, and a voice spoke softly.

"You are in need, my lord?" Samuel's voice asked.

"I am out of firewood, and my chambers grow cold," Coriander responded, not bothering to even turn in the direction of the young man.

"Apologies, sire. I will bring some up immediately." Without waiting for a response, the door closed.

Barely a handful of minutes passed before the door opened again, and the chamberlain appeared carrying a bundle of chopped firewood. Setting the bundle down, Samuel grabbed the poker and began to stir the embers, adding a pocket full of wood chips to entice the flames back to life. He began carefully stacking the cut logs on top.

Coriander watched him work in silence. The young man was plain in looks, but handsome in his own way. His sandy blond hair was unkempt, a sign he had been awakened by the prince's summons. He was of a lean build, his duties in the castle not physically demanding enough to allow him to develop obvious muscles. Yet there was something captivating about his presence.

He does have a cute butt, Coriander thought as Samuel leaned over to add another log to the fire, his shapely rear filling out his trousers.
The prince felt himself stirring below as he checked out Samuel, the heavy wool blanket hiding his growing desire.

It wasn't long before the fire roared back to life.

"I will bring up a few more logs, my lord," Samuel stated, his eyes not rising to meet Coriander's own.

"Please," Coriander replied in a soft tone to assure Samuel he held no anger toward the chamberlain for the empty woodpile.

Samuel nodded, quickly disappearing from the chambers again.

As the blazing fire began warming the chambers, Coriander found himself sweltering beneath the thick blanket. He let it drop to the floor and moved closer to the fire. The heat of the flames licked across his tanned skin. A slight sheen of sweat began to appear on his nude body, only to be instantly wicked away by the cool night breeze from the window. The competing sensations sent shivers through the prince's body.

There was a sudden loud clatter from the doorway. Coriander turned to see Samuel standing there, the young chamberlain's eyes blazing in the light from the fire. Several cut pieces of wood lay scattered about the floor at his feet. Coriander hadn't heard the door open.

"S-sorry, my lord," Samuel stammered, his eyes dropping away as he stooped to gather the scattered firewood. After a few awkward grasps, he had gathered the wood and carried it to the rack. The chamberlain began to carefully stack it in the holder, keeping his eyes firmly on his task.

As Samuel worked, Coriander's mind wandered. The memory of the stranger's green eyes haunted him, a constant reminder of his growing uncertainty. And then there was Leon—what would he think if he saw him now, seeking solace in the arms of a servant? But Coriander pushed those thoughts aside, focusing instead on the warmth spreading from the fire, the way it mirrored the slow burn in his chest.

Coriander watched Samuel, again struck by how attractive the young man was. Again his body began to react, his manhood beginning to stiffen with his increasingly lustful thoughts.

As Samuel finished stacking the wood, he rose and turned to the prince. "If there is nothing else, my lord," he stated, his eyes still downcast. He blushed suddenly, and his eyes did rise to meet Coriander's this time. They pointedly stayed looking upwards.

Coriander was suddenly aware of the throbbing desire in his body, particularly in certain parts of his body. He was certain it was the sight of his erect member that had brought the sudden blush to Samuel's face.

However, as he stared into the chamberlain's eyes, he saw a reflection of the same desire he himself felt.

"Do you like what you see?" Coriander whispered softly.

"I couldn't say, my lord." Samuel gulped, his eyes quickly darting down and back up. His blush deepened. "It wouldn't be proper."

Coriander hesitated, his gaze lingering on Samuel's downturned eyes. This wasn't like him—this impulsive need to reach out, to connect. But the emptiness he'd been feeling was too much, and Samuel was here, warm and real. He leaned in slowly, his breath mingling with the chamberlain's, a silent plea for something he couldn't quite name.

Coriander stepped closer to Samuel, a hair's breadth from his erection pressing into the man. He bent down to the slightly shorter chamberlain and brushed his lips against the man's.

Samuel's body stiffened in response, and then began to relax as his lips reacted and softly kissed the prince. Coriander chuckled seductively and kissed with a little more vigor. Samuel responded in kind.

The prince's breath came more rapidly as he reached out and grasped Samuel by the back of the neck. He pulled the young man against his body, his hard cock sliding up between them. The woolen fabric of Samuel's shirt sent pleasurable shivers through Coriander. Their kisses became deeper, and Samuel's hands began to explore the prince's body.

Coriander moaned slightly at the sensation. He began to tug at the chamberlain's shirt, and with a slight reprieve from the kissing, removed it. Their bodies pressed back together, and the warmth from Samuel's light skin burned into his own.

He pulled the young man down to the wool blanket he had discarded to the floor. Samuel enthusiastically complied. His kisses began to travel across the prince's neck and chest as they settled to the floor. Coriander moaned again as Samuel's lips traveled down his stomach and along his treasure trail.

Samuel wasted no more time on foreplay, as his warm breath was suddenly there and his tongue began to explore Coriander's slender and full length.

A burst of ecstasy flooded the prince's body, his back arching at the touch, and a strong moan escaped his lips. He was nearly certain he heard Samuel giggle at the outburst, but the thought was washed away as sudden warmth and wetness enveloped the head of his cock.

The prince was sure his eyes rolled back as the pleasure coursed through his body. At the very least, he knew his thighs had assumed a death grip against Samuel's ribs.

Samuel dutifully continued, his head moving up and down in a slow, teasing cadence as his mouth took in Coriander's fully erect length. Coriander's hips began to rock in time with Samuel's movements, his moans growing more frantic. Coriander's fingers slid through the young man's short hair, failing to find purchase.

Samuel's tempo began to increase, as his tongue teased the sensitive head of Coriander's cock on each upstroke. The prince's breathing became ragged as his body began to shake.
Coriander could feel the pressure building inside him. An almost burning sensation seemed to spread from his loins out into the tips of his fingers and toes. His head swam, and warmth flooded him as the dam finally broke.

He let out a low groan as his cock began to spasm. Samuel coughed, caught off guard at first, but after a moment matched the rhythm of the orgasm. His lips continued to work every drop of the warm liquid from the prince's nethers, as his throat happily devoured it.

It felt like ages before Coriander's body began to calm. He laid back on the wool blanket, his knees finally releasing Samuel from their vice-like grip. The chamberlain gasped for breath, lying his head on the prince's stomach. They stayed that way for several minutes, until their breathing had returned to normal.

Samuel placed a soft kiss against the prince's navel as he stood. He slid his shirt back on, pulling it down to cover his own apparent erection. His eyes roamed over Coriander's naked body one last time before meeting the prince's gaze.

"If there is nothing else, my lord?" he stated softly, before disappearing out the door without waiting for a response.

Coriander stared after him for a few moments, wondering if he should call the chamberlain back. He didn't feel quite right knowing the pleasure of the night had been so one-sided. But for whatever reason, it seemed Samuel was in a hurry to leave.

As Coriander pulled the blanket over himself, now warmed by the fire, he stared at the flickering lights across the ceiling, his mind a tangle of conflicting emotions. Had he taken things too far? Had he confused physical desire for something deeper?

As the warmth of the fire lulled him into a hazy calm, Coriander's mind raced. Was this what he wanted? Or had he simply sought comfort in the easiest way he knew how?

Chapter Ten

Another week passed before Coriander could return to the forest. Harsh storms had rolled across the kingdom the past few days, leaving the landscape damp and muddy. Thankfully, this day was clear and bright with warm sunlight, although a chill breeze announced the approaching autumn.

He wore heavier clothes than usual to combat the cool breeze and what was sure to be a cold night. His look was completed with a fur-lined heavy cloak of forest green, to ward off the rain should the weather turn again.

The loose curls of his hair drifted with the breeze as he and Zedd traveled, making him wish he had trimmed it before heading out. The muddy roads made travel slower than he would have liked, and he had to be even more careful once he turned off the main path. The grassy, rock-strewn hills he had to traverse to reach the forest posed a real danger to Zedd, and Coriander would much prefer not to lame his horse so far from civilization.

Despite these setbacks, the prince arrived at his usual camping spot a couple of hours after midday. The sun still gave plenty of light to the area, but the air was much cooler here.

Coriander worked methodically, his fingers numb from the cold as he brushed down Zedd and fed him an apple. The fire took longer to coax to life than usual, the damp wood reluctant to catch. When the first flames finally flickered to life, he felt a small sense of accomplishment, though it did little to warm the chill in his bones.

Next, he set up his tent, close enough to the fire to get some benefit from its warmth, but not close enough to risk an errant ember setting it ablaze. He laid out his bedroll atop a thick blanket to protect it from the damp ground and stowed the rest of his gear in the corner.

He carefully selected a small bag from the gear, slipping the single thin strap over his shoulder. The contents rang together slightly as they clicked into each other.

Assured his camp was safely prepared, he strapped his sword to his belt and headed off into the forest.

By this point, he was certain he could find the little grotto while blind and in the dark. His visits to it had worn the deer path into a footpath. The way was easier, with less underbrush and obstacles in the path.

The forest was alive with the scents of damp earth and decaying leaves, the air crisp with the promise of autumn. The trees, heavy with moisture, dripped steadily, each drop echoing in the stillness. The sky above was a bright, endless blue, but the chill in the air warned of colder days to come.

Soon he could hear the bubbling water of the little waterfall. It had a more furious cadence than normal, and soon Coriander saw why. The recent rains had swelled the little brook feeding the waterfall, and the water now poured down into the small pond rather than the peaceful trickle it had been before.

The pond itself had suffered from the rains too, with the water now flooded up beyond the reeds lining its edge. It was more murky now, with more of a brown color than the normally crystal-clear waters typically filling it.

He paused, listening to the forest around him, half-expecting to hear the rustle of wings or the soft footfalls of the stranger. But the only sound was the bubbling brook and the distant call of a bird. He sighed, the weight of his hopes settling heavily on his shoulders as he reluctantly turned back toward camp.

He set the small bag down next to the rock outcropping from which the waterfall cascaded. From it, he pulled two small containers and a bright red cloth. The small sealed glass carafe of milk settled into a small eddy in the brook. The water would keep the fresh liquid cool.

Next, he laid the red cloth on the rocks beside the carafe, and on top of it, he placed a small clay jar. The top was sealed with red wax bearing the crest of the royal apiary.

Finally, he produced a small square of stiff paper from his pocket and leaned it against the honey jar. In a simple but elegant script, it stated: *'Gifts given freely, with no obligation.'*

He adjusted the items a few times, fussing over their presentation. Finally, mostly satisfied, he slung the empty bag back over his shoulder and returned to camp.

Shadows were beginning to creep over the camp as the sun started its trek towards evening. Coriander fed some more damp wood to the fire. He set the small pot on the edge of the embers and filled it from his water skin, followed by a few fresh vegetables, dried meat, and spices.

He sat on a blanket by the fire, lost in thought. Would the stranger—the fairy—accept his gifts? Had he already left, never to be seen again? Around and around, these thoughts and others passed through the prince's mind, until finally, the smell of the soup pulled him from his contemplations.

As he stirred the soup, Coriander's thoughts drifted to the castle, to the responsibilities waiting for him there. Every hour he spent chasing shadows in the forest pulled him further from his duties, from the future his father had meticulously planned for him. But the pull of the stranger, of those green eyes, was too strong to resist. He knew he was treading dangerous ground, but the uncertainty and thrill of it all made it impossible to turn away.

Lifting the pot with care by its delicate handle, he moved it away from the embers, ensuring it stayed close to the fire for warmth.

As the shadows deepened, he ignored his grumbling stomach, rising to gather his belongings before venturing back into the forest.

At the grotto, his heart sank at the sight of the untouched gifts. The carafe and clay jar sat exactly as he had left them, their bright colors almost mocking him in the fading light. He stared at them for a long moment, a mix of frustration and sorrow bubbling up within him. Walking back to camp was a melancholy experience. He knew he was being too hard on himself. The stranger was a creature of myth, after all. Surely no lowly mortal could ever attract its attention. Was he foolish to think such a being would care for such offerings?

Despite no longer having an appetite, Coriander ate anyway. There was no enjoyment in the act, and his mood made the soup seem bland and unfulfilling.

The forest felt impossibly vast and empty, the silence pressing in on him as he sat alone by the fire. His thoughts circled endlessly around the stranger, around Leon, around the growing distance between himself and everything he had once known. Even the warmth of the flames couldn't chase away the cold that settled deep within him.

He could almost hear Leon's voice in his head, chastising him for abandoning his duties. "*You're too serious, Cory. You need to focus on what's real, not chase after fairy tales.*" But what did Leon know about this gnawing emptiness? Coriander shook his head, trying to banish the thought, but the words lingered, echoing in the quiet of the forest.

He hung a bag of oats on the tree for Zedd, cleaned up the campsite, dumped some more wood on the fire, and crawled into his tent as the last bit of orange and purple light faded from the sky.

As the fire crackled softly beside him, Coriander pulled the fur cloak tighter around himself. The night was colder than he had anticipated, and despite the snug bedroll, he couldn't seem to shake the chill that had taken root inside him. His thoughts lingered on the stranger, the unanswered questions gnawing at him as he drifted into a restless sleep, wondering if he would ever see those impossibly green eyes again.

    Just as sleep began to claim him, a faint rustle reached his ears, almost indistinguishable from the sounds of the forest. His eyes snapped open, heart pounding as he strained to hear it again. Was it just the wind, or something more? For a moment, he lay there, listening, but the sound didn't return. Yet the unease lingered, gnawing at him until exhaustion finally pulled him under.

Chapter Eleven

The milk and honey were gone!

Coriander's heart leapt with joy. The spring had returned to its normal size and flow, the excess water finally having receded. On the rocks where he had left the honey, the red cloth still sat, but the clay jar was gone. The carafe was also missing.

The red cloth had been folded neatly, and the paper card with the prince's note was inside it. The note hadn't changed, but it had been wrapped in the cloth with what felt like reverence. He pocketed the note and cloth, his thoughts racing. Although the banks of the spring had returned to normal, the ground around the reeds was still a muddy mess, a lingering reminder of the recent upheaval. And there! Between the reeds, in the opening to the spring, were two distinct footprints.

Coriander wasn't the worst tracker in the kingdom, but he had to hope that person didn't die. Only a few feet past the footprints, he had already lost the tracks. This is why he preferred hunting with snares; the animals came to you.

Not that he was comparing the stranger to an animal! He shook the thought from his head. But the gifts had been accepted! This meant the stranger was still around!

That's what it has to mean! Sure, someone else could have taken the milk and honey, but given the rich make of the cloth, no one else would have left it behind.

He checked the grotto several more times throughout the day, yet he found no other signs of the stranger. As the sun began to set, the depressing weight of failure once again settled across his shoulders.

By nightfall, a warm breeze blew through the air, accompanied by a cool mist and a few errant raindrops. It was looking like a rainy night.

Coriander stowed everything in the tent and made sure Zedd was taken care of. Then he sealed himself inside the tent, tying the flap closed securely. Just as he completed his task, the wind picked up and the tempo of the rain changed to a downpour.

Not feeling up to much else, he snuffed his lantern and went to sleep.

The howl awoke him. The cloth of the tent flapped madly about him as the vicious wind roared past. Nearby, the sound of splintering wood as a tree crashed to the earth. Distantly, he heard a distressed call from Zedd.

Coriander quickly pulled on boots, having slept dressed, and wrapped his cloak around his shoulders. He had just finished fastening it when a great tearing sound came from the tent. The sewn seams split, and the storm came in.

The wind was a beast, slamming into Coriander's chest like a hammer and throwing him to the ground. Nearly every item in the tent was tossed away, even his bedroll lifted into the air and disappeared into the darkness.

He was almost certain he screamed in rage, but the storm's fury was louder. The wind stole his breath away and deafened his shout. With all the willpower he could muster, he stood in defiance of the storm. Pulling his cloak tight to his body, he leaned into the wind and rain and took a single step forward.

The wind accepted his challenge, howling madly as it redoubled its efforts. The prince's feet slid in the wet grass, but he remained standing.

Again, trees crashed down nearby in the darkness. Somewhere far off, he was sure he again heard the whinny of Zedd, seeming to reach him through the wind. He began to stumble one step at a time as he moved in the direction of his lost horse.

This was no ordinary storm, but one of the great storms that sometimes rolled in from the sea. Coriander had not seen one since he was a boy. The castle stood up well against it, but he still remembered riding with his father among the town and countryside afterward. Homes had been torn apart, land was flooded, and many people had lost their lives.

"Courage isn't about not being afraid, Cory," his father's voice echoed in his memory, from that stormy day years ago. *"It's about doing what needs to be done, even when you're terrified."* Those words pushed him forward now, driving him to take another step, and then another.

The prince pushed on. Between the blasts of wind and driving rain, his cloak seemed useless. Especially considering half the time he couldn't even keep it wrapped around him. Loose debris pelted him relentlessly—small sticks, branches, and even an entire bush slammed against him, each impact driving the breath from his lungs. Soon, he was soaked, bruised, and bleeding in more than one place.

More than once, the wind or debris knocked him to the ground, and he struggled in the mud to stand again. Trees still crashed regularly about the forest, at least one coming dangerously close to his path.

Somehow, again reaching him over the wind's anger, he heard the neighing of Zedd. It seemed closer, and less distressed. All his efforts pushed him to follow the sound.

Another devastating blast of wind struck him, nearly knocking him off his feet. He fought to stay upright, but the wind was relentless. With a vicious tug, it ripped his cloak free, tearing away a chunk of his shirt with it, leaving him exposed to the elements.

Even as he fought the storm, Coriander couldn't shake the feeling that he was being watched, that somewhere in the darkness, the stranger was waiting. It was this thought that drove him forward, despite the storm's fury, despite the pain that coursed through his battered body.

Ahead, he must be hallucinating, he could make out a thin strand of light in the heavy rain. He staggered toward it, his strength nearly spent, willpower slipping away with every labored step. Desperation gnawed at him—he had to reach that light, or he might never see daylight again.

Suddenly, the storm around him seemed to fall away. The rain became a soft and steady patter against his head and back. The wind was now a gentle whisper, a stark contrast to the raging tempest just beyond his reach. The storm seemed to claw at the edges of this strange sanctuary, as if furious that he had escaped its grasp.

A rise of bare rock greeted him ahead, a soft warm glow shining out from a crevice between the stones. The opening was disguised well, and he doubted even in the daylight he would have been able to find it without the aiding amber light. It was small, but wide enough that even a horse could squeeze through without much struggle.

As he slipped inside, he heard Zedd greet him ahead, and outside, the storm crashed down again as if released from whatever had been holding it back.

The cavern was small but surprisingly welcoming, the warmth from the fire filling the space with a comforting glow. The stone walls were rough, yet the light danced across them in a way that made them seem almost alive. It was a stark contrast to the fury that raged just outside—a safe haven carved out of the wild, a place where the storm's reach could not extend.

He scraped his face against an outcropping of rock and banged his shin into another before stumbling into the open cavern. Zedd gave another whinny of greeting upon seeing him. A warm fire crackled in the center of the open space, casting flickering shadows on the walls. Just before his vision faded, Coriander caught a glimpse of something—no, someone. A flash of red hair. His heart leapt even as his body gave out, collapsing into the welcoming darkness.

Chapter Twelve

Coriander's eyes fluttered open after an indeterminate amount of time. He lay comfortably close to the fire, but his clothes were still soaking wet. Not much time could have passed. He started to sit up, but his head swam, and he immediately lay back down. Something wet but soft was under his head. Reaching up, he realized his cloak was folded underneath him, though pieces of his shirt still hung from the clasps.

Instead of trying to rise again, he looked around as best he could. Zedd was nearby, munching contentedly from his feed bag, which hung from some rocks. Coriander wondered where that had come from.

On the other side of the fire was a pile of leaves and pine needles, gathered together in the rough shape of a bed. Beside the pile sat the empty carafe and a clay jar.

Without thinking, Coriander sat up quickly at the sight and immediately regretted it. Dizziness washed over him, and his stomach threatened to revolt. He steadied himself with one hand against the warm stone floor and took several deep breaths until the dizziness subsided.

He peeled off his torn shirt, the fabric clinging to his skin like a second layer of sodden rags. As the fire's warmth kissed his bare skin, a shiver ran down his spine, the contrasting sensations of heat and lingering dampness leaving him both comforted and unsettled. He kicked off his boots next, setting them close to the fire. After some thought, his pants followed too. He sat there on the bare and warm stone floor in just his damp loincloth, feeling the aches in his body from the storm's harsh embrace.

Listening carefully, Coriander noticed that the storm's ferocity seemed to have lessened. Perhaps it had already passed? Just how long had he been out?

Shakily, Coriander rose to his feet. A sharp pain shot through his shin where a bad bruise had formed, causing him to hobble for the first few steps. Despite the fire's warmth, a deep-seated chill lingered in his bones, a reminder of the storm that had nearly claimed him.

As he approached the cave's entrance, the stranger appeared.

He was still as naked as ever, except for Coriander's pack and sword that he carried. The stranger froze as his eyes locked onto the prince's, all but for a tightening of his grip on the sword.

"Do not attempt to leave," the stranger spoke in his soft voice. "It may appear calm, but it is a deception. The storm's center is above us; a watching eye to lead the foolish into false hope."

He must have seen some understanding in Coriander's eyes, as he gave a gentle nod and stepped past the prince. The stranger set the pack next to Coriander's boots by the fire, but leaned the sword against the cave wall next to his leaf bed.

"Your pack seems to have some food that wasn't spoiled by the weather. You must be hungry. Please eat." He settled himself down on the bedding.

His body up close was even more beautiful than Coriander remembered. His finely toned muscles were perfectly suited to his frame, every line seeming crafted by a master artist. His face had a haunting symmetry to it, save for a small mole near his left eye.

His hair was a nearly unnatural shade of red, invoking thoughts of strawberries and roses. It had been trimmed since Coriander had last seen him, now short and neat. His apple-green eyes seemed to be sizing the prince up in a similar fashion, though there was a flicker of something deeper—an ancient wisdom that belied his youthful appearance.

Below a bit of red bush, his slender and soft manhood rested invitingly across one thigh.

"You're beautiful," Coriander blurted out. Those piercing green eyes rose to meet his, flashing something like anger.

"Do not presume to tarry thy tongue with honeyed words, mortal." The warning was harsh and carried a weight behind the words that made Coriander's breath catch.

Coriander's eyes dropped to the stone. He spread out his cloak and sat up on it, dragging his pack over. The soggy mess of bread wasn't even worth trying to save. The dried meats weren't quite so dry anymore, but were still fine to eat. The same was true of the cheese, a bottle of wine that had somehow survived, and a small collection of apples.

Zedd neighed softly next to Coriander's ear, startling him. The horse nudged his shoulder. The prince laughed, holding up one of the treats for his mount. Zedd took it graciously, crunching on it happily with a thankful gleam in his eye.

"Your beast has great love for you in his heart," the stranger spoke. "It was his idea to bring you here." Zedd shook his mane and snorted loudly. The stranger smiled warmly at the stallion. "He was very insistent."

"So if my horse hadn't vouched for me, you'd have let the storm kill me?"

Coriander asked, his voice tinged with curiosity and a hint of challenge. The stranger seemed to take a deep breath, as if calming himself before speaking. His words were dry and clipped.

"I do not mourn the loss of those whose axes reap our forests, and whose hammers break our mountains."

"Then why save me from the bandit?" Coriander responded. The stranger met his eyes, a glimmer of something there—regret? Disdain?—before he resumed drinking, the moment gone as quickly as it had appeared.

"He threatened your horse."

Coriander couldn't help himself. He laughed at the absurdity of it all. Outside, the wind began to howl against the cave mouth, spouting its displeasure that it couldn't reach the occupants.

"The storm should pass fully within a few hours," the stranger said, seeming to respond to an unasked question by the prince. "Worry not, you are safe here."

"Am I?" Coriander's gaze fell to his sword beside the stranger. Again, he received that sly smile.

"You have my guarantee of safety, under the Laws of Hospitality." The slight edge of humor faded from his gaze. "Assuming you act like a proper guest."

Coriander swallowed hard, the weight of the man's words pressing down on him. The threat was not just implied; it was palpable, hanging in the air like the charged atmosphere before a storm. He truly believed the stranger would make good on those words if necessary.

"Well, let me introduce myself. I am Pr—"

"Prince Coriander," the stranger interrupted, "son of King Eric and the late Queen Abigail. I know who you are, Prince," he inflected the word heavily, "and neither your titles nor the depths of your coin purse impress me."

"That's not being very hospitable," Coriander muttered. The stranger was on his feet in an instant.

"*Excuse* me?!" His words were hard and sharp, trembling with anger. But this time Coriander wasn't shaken. He was a prince after all. Decorum and hospitality had been drilled into him since a young age.

"Is it not proper for a host to introduce themselves to a guest?" Coriander asked simply, no challenge in his tone. The stranger shook with anger a moment more, then visibly calmed with another deep breath.

"You walk a fine line, prince." His expression softened. "You may call me Shyne of Clematis."

Coriander bowed the best he could while seated. "It is a pleasure to make your acquaintance, Shyne."

"Shyne," he said in a corrective tone. Coriander didn't hear a difference in how he had pronounced it, but another repeat seemed to satisfy the fairy.

"Clematis? Aren't those the red flowers that spring up in the fields during summer?" Shyne nodded.

"Yes, those of which I was born."

"You're born from flowers?" Coriander hadn't read any such thing in his books.

"Simply: yes. However, it is far more complicated than that. Now, no more questions. Eat." As he sat back down on his bedding, his hands motioned for Coriander to do the same.

Coriander obliged. Despite having been soaked by the rain, the cured meat was tough and tasteless. The cheese was a step better, but he was hungry enough that he didn't care either way.

"Want some?" Coriander offered it to Shyne. The fairy glared at the food with disdain.

"We do not require sustenance as you mortals do," he replied tartly, shifting his position on the bed. Coriander couldn't help but notice as Shyne's member flopped to the other thigh. "We only eat for the pleasure of it. To savor the tastes and flavors."

Coriander shrugged and went back to eating. After a moment, he asked, "The milk and honey?"

Shyne's lips almost cracked into a smile. "A pleasant gift. Sweet and rich, simple products of nature herself."

The prince did smile, thinking that maybe he had figured out how this game was played. The cork came free of the wine bottle with a satisfying pop. He held the bottle out in invitation.

Leaning forward slightly, Shyne's nostrils flared as he sniffed the air. "A sweet red, dry and aged to perfection." He nodded approval. "I will partake." He picked up the glass carafe and leaned closer to the prince.

"It's from the Silverthorne winery," Coriander replied as he began pouring the deep red liquid into the carafe. "The best in the kingdom. This particular bottle has aged seven years."

The wine roughly split between them, Shyne sat back and sipped from the carafe. The light of pleasure in his eyes was immediately apparent to Coriander. The prince grinned.

"Best in the kingdom!" he repeated enthusiastically.

"Certainly worthy of that praise." Shyne gave a slow nod of approval as he took a second sip.

They sat in silence after that, finishing the wine between them. Coriander completed his meal and did what he could to make sure Zedd was comfortable.

"Get some rest, Prince Coriander. I will awaken you when the storm has passed."

Coriander doubted he would find rest, his mind swirling with thoughts of Shyne and the strange events that had led him here. Yet, as he laid his head against the mostly dried cloak, the warmth of the fire and the weight of his exhaustion pulled him into a restless slumber, where dreams and reality blurred into one.

Chapter Thirteen

With a stiff groan, Coriander sat up. The rocky floor had not been the greatest place to sleep. Faint birdsong reached his ears from the cave opening. It seemed the storm was finally gone.

He glanced over at Shyne. The fairy was soundlessly asleep, curled up on the leafy bedding. A pang tugged at his heart as he watched the peaceful rise and fall of Shyne's chest. There was something incredibly endearing about the way he slept, his face serene and untroubled.

Coriander stood and, as silently as possible, began packing the few things he had left. With the storm broken, he knew search parties would be out looking for him.

Shyne had recovered most of Zedd's gear. With everything else packed away on the horse, all that remained was his sword. It still sat propped against the wall by Shyne's bed.

A few silent steps brought him to the fairy's side. He stopped just before reaching for the sword. From this angle, he had a clearer view of Shyne's back. Long, thin, curving lines covered his upper back like faded tattoos. After a moment's study, Coriander realized they matched the gossamer wings he had seen spring from Shyne's back before.

His fingers itched to trace the delicate lines on Shyne's back, a part of him yearning for that connection. But even as the desire pulled at him, he knew it would be a violation of the quiet trust they had built—a line he wasn't willing to cross without Shyne's consent.

So instead, he lifted his sword and returned to Zedd. The scabbard was missing, but he managed to secure the blade to his pack where it wouldn't be a danger to him or the horse. However, this also meant he wouldn't be able to draw it quickly if needed.

Taking Zedd's lead, they headed toward the cave's exit. Just as Coriander was about to duck outside, Shyne's voice cut through the silence, making the prince pause and turn.

"Do not return, Prince Coriander." Shyne's bright green eyes burned into him with a serious fire. "You will not find this place again."

Coriander gave him a silent nod and a smile of appreciation. Then he squeezed through the narrow exit, leading Zedd behind him.

Morning birds chirped cheerily in the crisp dawn air, their song a stark contrast to the devastation around them. The ground was a soggy mess of mud and fallen leaves, broken branches scattered like remnants of a forgotten battle. The storm had left its mark on the forest, and Coriander could see where the once-beautiful landscape had been marred by its fury.

In an effort to maintain some semblance of propriety, Coriander dressed in his torn pants and tattered shirt. They were still a step above being in just his loincloth, but only by a bare margin.

His heart tightened as he passed the area of the grotto. It was completely flooded, now looking more like a small lake than the tiny pond it had once been. Part of the rocky outcropping had collapsed, and the rush of water from the overtaxed brook now spilled down its side rather than into the waters. Coriander was unsure if any of it would return to the natural wonder it had been before.

As Coriander led Zedd through the ruined forest, the weight of his responsibilities pressed down on him. The devastation around him was a stark reminder of his inability to protect his people, and the memory of Shyne's parting words lingered in his mind, a nagging doubt that he couldn't shake. How could he reconcile his duty to his kingdom with the strange, powerful pull he felt toward the fairy? And where did that leave Samuel, who offered him a different kind of comfort, but comfort nonetheless?

He was nearly out of the woods when he first heard the signal whistle. Three sharp notes echoed through the air to meet him. He didn't remember seeing the whistle Leon had given him among his things, so he shouted instead.

"Here!" he called out as loudly as he could, pulling Zedd to follow as he headed in the direction of the whistle. Its sound likely carried much farther than his voice could, and any rescue party probably wasn't close enough to hear him.

After a few more minutes of walking, he reached the edge of the woods and came into view of the ridge that led up to the main roads. Much of it had been washed away, leaving muddy scars down its once grassy surface.

At the top of the ridge sat a stark white horse with a black diamond on its chest. Its rider scanned the woodline further down with a spyglass.

"Here!" Coriander called again, his voice cracking in relief.

At the sound of his call, Leon spotted him, tossed the spyglass to the ground, and leapt from Gemstone's back. He half-tumbled and slid down the muddy ridge, hitting the bottom at a run. Not even slowing down, he crashed into the prince and threw his arms around him.

"Cory!" he cried out in a tight voice as Coriander returned his embrace. Leon squeezed his friend tightly, until the prince finally let out a struggling breath of protest.

"Air!" Coriander gasped. Leon laughed, the weight of relief evident. He released his friend, and Coriander drew in a deep breath.

Leon turned, raising a signal whistle to his lips. He blew a long, piercing note, waited a few heartbeats, and then repeated it.

"We thought the worst." Leon turned back to his friend. Moisture had gathered at the corner of his eye.

"It took me by surprise," Coriander said, indicating his ruined clothing, "but I managed to find shelter."

Other riders had begun to appear at the top of the ridge. More knights of the realm. Zedd neighed in greeting to the familiar friends they rode on, and many answered his call.

Leon's roguish grin lit up his face, a familiar expression that brought some comfort to Coriander's weary heart. "Let's get you back home, sire," Leon said, his tone carrying the weight of everything they had endured.

The trip home was a depressing one. The great storm had ravaged the land. Crop fields were flooded and destroyed. Almost no homes had escaped damage, with some gone altogether.
One small village was gone completely, only a few stones of the foundations and the road running between them the only indication any civilization had ever been there at all.

"The city escaped the worst of it," Leon explained as they rode. "The high walls around the capital seemed to break the winds enough to keep damage to a minimum. But as you've seen, many of the villages and towns weren't so lucky."

Coriander remained silent, absorbing the destruction and loss around him. Seeing the ruined village, Coriander felt a mix of anger and helplessness rise within him. He had been raised to protect his people, yet here was evidence of how little he could truly do against the forces of nature. And now, with his father's decree, he was more a prisoner than a prince—a prisoner of duty and circumstance.

Leon continued, "Your father already has the knights combing the area, looking for those who can be assisted and assessing damages. He has sent out a call to all craftsmen and opened the kingdom's coffers to aid in repairs and rebuilding."

A small grunt of acknowledgment was all the prince managed. Finally, they crested the last hill, and the capital came into sight. The granite stone walls and towering spires were a welcome relief to Coriander. The castle loomed on the horizon, its stone walls rising like a fortress against the chaos of the world outside. To Coriander, it had always been a place of safety, but now, as he approached its gates, it felt more like a cage—a reminder of the duties and expectations that kept him bound. His heart soared at the sight of home, but a shadow of doubt lingered.

Coriander stormed into his chambers, slamming the door behind him. The sound echoed in the room, startling Samuel into dropping his dust bin. The scattered dirt mirrored the chaos in Coriander's mind—anger, frustration, and helplessness all fighting for control.

"How dare he!" the prince roared to no one in particular, having not even noticed Samuel. "I am not a child to still bend to his bidding!" With a furious cry, he swept the books and papers from his desk to the floor.

"'Can't leave the city!'" he mocked in a pompous tone. "'Too dangerous for the only heir.'"

Samuel cleared his throat lightly, casting his eyes to the floor and squeaking out a quiet, "Sire."

Coriander spun, his fury finding a target. He stomped over to the servant, nearly growling in rage. Samuel flinched at his approach, but kept his eyes turned downward.
Something in Coriander broke at the sight of the cowering chamberlain, and his anger washed away. He had never intentionally mistreated any of the castle's many servants, and he wasn't going to let his anger at his father allow him to start now.

"Oh Samuel," the prince whispered, embracing the young man. Samuel stiffened at the unexpected contact. "I am so sorry." Coriander released him and stepped back. "Please forgive me. My anger was not for you."

"Yes, sire." Samuel's eyes timidly met the prince's. "May I please return to my duties?"

"Please." Coriander turned and began collecting the books and papers he had scattered. There was no reason to add extra work for the chamberlain. Samuel, for his part, stooped and began sweeping the scattered dirt back into the dustbin.

His mess cleaned, Coriander laid back in his bed, fuming at the ceiling. His father had forbidden him from leaving the city again without permission, and certainly without escort. So now, even if he wanted to pursue Shyne, he couldn't.

After a while of furious thoughts, he heard Samuel quietly clear his throat again. "Any other needs, my lord?"

Turning to the young man, Coriander saw his eyes were cast downward again, but that couldn't hide the creeping blush on his cheeks and neck.

"Lie with me." Coriander surprised himself by saying.

"Sire... are you sure?" There was a vulnerability in his voice that Coriander hadn't heard before, a quiet plea for reassurance that this meant more than just a command.

"Lie with me," Coriander repeated. "I will cover for you with the steward."

Hesitantly, Samuel complied. He climbed into the bed next to the prince, his back turned towards him and a few precious inches separating them.

Coriander turned on his side, negating those few inches of space. He slid his arm around Samuel's chest and pulled him close. "Thank you," he whispered into the young man's ear, barely a breath of sound.

As Coriander lay in bed, his arm draped over Samuel's chest, a sense of unease settled over him. This moment of peace felt fragile, temporary, as if it could be shattered by the slightest change in the wind. He couldn't help but wonder what the future held—whether his choices now would lead him down a path he couldn't escape.

Later, when Coriander was snoring lightly, Samuel slipped from his grasp. He stood for a few moments, staring down at the sleeping prince. A small, shy smile graced his face, and he quietly left the room to return to his duties.

Chapter Fourteen

Two weeks had passed since the great storm, and the kingdom was slowly returning to a semblance of normalcy. The scars of the disaster were still visible in the streets, but the people had begun to rebuild. In the market district, a white marble monolith was being erected—a solemn memorial to those lost or still missing. The names of the dead were being painstakingly carved into its surface, a reminder of the lives that had been forever changed.

Despite the heavy atmosphere, the king had announced a massive festival, hoping to bring some cheer back to the land. Once again, coins flowed from the royal coffers to fund it all. Town criers were sent far and wide to spread the word, inviting entertainers, merchants, and anyone else who wished to attend. The main attraction was to be a jousting tournament with a hefty prize promised to the winner.

That weekend, the kingdom was packed wall to wall with its citizens.

Coriander's mood had lightened somewhat, though the restrictions confining him to the capital city still chafed. Even so, he couldn't resist the excitement of a festival this massive.

He walked the venue with Leon at his side as his protection. The past weeks had repaired their friendship, and as they strolled about, they watched the attractions and generally behaved like children half their age.

The festival was a kaleidoscope of colors and sounds. Banners in the kingdom's vibrant colors fluttered in the breeze, the fabric snapping lightly as it caught the wind. The rich aroma of roasting meat mingled with the sweetness of pastries, tempting the senses and drawing the crowd deeper into the celebration. Musicians played lively tunes on every corner, their melodies weaving through the laughter and chatter that filled the streets.

But as Coriander walked with Leon, a sense of unease settled in his chest. He couldn't pinpoint why, but something about the day felt off. Leon, usually so confident, seemed distracted. Coriander shook off the feeling, telling himself it was nothing—but the shadow of doubt lingered.

Leon chucked the small ball with all his strength. It shot through the air with deadly precision, striking its target with killing intent. With a hollow echo, it bounced off the stacked clay jars and landed on the ground with a disappointed thud. The clay jars barely even wiggled.

"Rigged!" Leon shouted, as Coriander burst into uproarious laughter. "Either rigged or witchcraft!"

The game vendor offered Leon another ball, another chance for just a copper coin. Leon fumed but slammed another coin on the table and took the ball. Another throw. Another failure. More laughter from Coriander.

"How?!" The righteous indignation dropped from the knight's voice. The vendor shrugged, reached over, and pushed the clay jars. They tumbled to the ground easily. He restacked them and offered another ball to Leon.

But the knight was done. He stormed off, muttering about witches and conmen. Coriander followed, finally getting his laughter down to a light cackle.

"The mighty knight, Sir Leon! Felled by a carnival game!" Coriander teased.

Leon shot him a mockingly dangerous glare, but there was a flicker of something else on his face—concern, perhaps? "And how many coins did he filch from you, my Prince?"

Coriander's eyes dropped. "Eleven," he muttered.

"Pre-cise-ly." Leon enunciated each syllable, but his voice softened as if his mind was already on the upcoming tournament.

A bell tolled out across the square, saving Coriander from any further teasing. It was the announcement that the tournament would be starting soon.

They walked together to the large tent that had been erected near the stadium to serve as a combat barracks for the tournament participants. They wished each other luck and parted ways.

Several smaller competitions had been set up before the main jousting tournament. One of those was a swordsman's duel.

Coriander stood across from his opponent, some Duke or Lord's son whose name he hadn't bothered to learn. The clash of swords and the cheers of the crowd were supposed to invigorate him, but instead, they left a bitter taste in his mouth. What was the point of all this showmanship, when lives could be lost for sport? Yet, here he was, just another player in the game.

So far, neither had landed a strike on the other, and the crowd was eating up the suspense.

The other man stepped forward suddenly, the light of the sun gleaming off his breastplate as he moved—the only armor either man wore. The overhead blow was fast, but the prince had expected it and was faster.

He sidestepped the blow and turned the momentum into a forward strike, aimed at his opponent's breast. The man shifted his weight, pulled his trajectory, and managed to strike Coriander's sword away at the last moment.

The maneuver put the man off balance; however, Coriander pressed the advantage. Facing a flurry of blows, the man chose to evade. He turned his unsteady balance into a roll, putting distance between himself and the prince. He came back to his feet, ready to defend an incoming blow.

Coriander pursued the retreating man, anticipated his defense, and struck. He caught the man's sword on his, spun it to break his opponent's grip, and the weapon soared away. Before the man could recover, the tip of Coriander's blade pressed on his throat.

The swords they used were real, but unsharpened. While a blow could break bone, it was rare they drew blood. But the man knew regardless that he was beaten.

"Yield!" he cried out.

The crowd went wild. Flags bearing the kingdom's colors and crest waved wildly in the air. Coriander saluted the people to their enthusiastic cheering, then traded grips with the other man. They walked back to the barracks tent together.

Behind him, Coriander heard the crowd calm as the crier announced the next event: the jousting tournament.

Coriander arrived on the raised dais in the middle of his father's speech, having taken the opportunity to clean up and change back into his royal finery. He wore a red overcoat trimmed in gold embroidery over a ruffled white shirt. Trousers in a deep blue completed the outfit. He took a seat in one of the smaller chairs to the side and behind his father's temporary throne just as his speech was wrapping up.

"...and that is why we will always rise to each challenge," the king's voice boomed across the crowd, "because in troubled times we stand together.

Indivisible. Unbreaking." The crowd cheered, and his father allowed the elation to continue for a few moments before gesturing for silence. He was a well-practiced statesman, and knew how to manipulate a crowd.

"So for those that cannot be here today," he continued in a solemn tone, "we shall do the living for them!" His voice crescendoed to another roar from the crowd.

"Today we salute those who fight for us, and lay down their lives for our safety," he shouted over the roar of the crowd. "The knights of this realm and of our neighbors shall show us the strength of their will and the courage of their hearts!"

From somewhere, several trumpeters played out a few sharp notes as the king roared, "Let the tournament begin!"

The festival was a spectacle of sound and color as the first two contestants rode out onto the field. But Coriander wasn't paying them any attention. Instead, his eyes were focused on the back of his father's head. He was still angry at the restrictions that had been placed upon him, so he sat fuming in silence.

He heard the crowd cheering as one of the knights scored enough points to win. Coriander snapped out of his dark gloom as he heard Leon's name announced for the next round. He sat forward in his seat in anticipation.

The other knight rode out first, clad in full plate armor that had been stained black. His shield and lance were both solid black, with the exception of the former being painted with a golden eagle. To top off the egregious look, his stallion was also solid black. He was from the house of one of the competing lords.

Leon came out next, his armor nearly the complete opposite of the other knight. His armor shone nearly mirror-bright. His shield bore the kingdom's crest, and his lance was a spiral of alternating red and gold stripes. He was astride one of the kingdom's many warhorses, opting to spare Gemstone from the possible dangers of the tournament.

The knights sat across from one another, pure symbols of strength and nobility upon the backs of their beautiful steeds. They raised their lances in salute of each other, as a hushed silence fell over the crowd.

The flags dropped, and for a heartbeat, everything was still. Then the horses surged forward, muscles rippling under glistening armor. Each stride brought the knights closer, their lances lowering with deliberate precision. Time stretched, the distance between them narrowing, until the inevitable collision that would decide their fates.

The ground trembled beneath the thunderous charge of the horses, each powerful stride sending vibrations up through Coriander's boots. The pounding of hooves was like a drumbeat, matched by the rhythmic chants of the crowd, who held their breath in anticipation of the coming clash.

Coriander held his breath as Leon's lance struck his opponent with a force that echoed through the stadium. Splinters flew as the black knight was nearly unseated, his shield arm trembling under the impact. The shattered lance lay in pieces on the ground, each fragment a reminder of how easily strength could be undone.

The doctors checked on the black knight, who was holding his shield arm but seemed otherwise fine.

The tournament continued, Leon winning each of his matches and climbing the match ladder. Soon it was the semifinals, and then it happened.

As Leon and his newest opponent clashed, the opponent's lance glanced off Leon's shield and slid upwards. It shattered across the side of his helmet, knocking it off his head and sending Leon tumbling to the ground. The crowd gasped.

For a moment, Coriander thought Leon might stand up. He held his breath, watching for any sign of movement. But then, as the doctors reached him, Coriander saw the blood—so much blood. The realization hit like a physical blow, knocking the wind out of him. Leon wasn't moving. Leon wasn't... No. He couldn't even finish the thought. The shock of it paralyzed him, freezing him in place as the world around him crumbled.

"Leon!" he cried, leaping from the dais before he even realized he had moved. The world around him blurred as he raced toward his fallen friend, his pulse pounding in his ears. The doctors reached Leon first, their frantic movements only heightening Coriander's fear. He struggled against the Knight Marshall's grip, desperate to get closer, but the sight of Leon's bloodied face stopped him cold. The red stain spreading across the ground was a stark reminder of how fragile life could be.

Coriander stood frozen, the shouts of the crowd distant and muffled, like he was underwater. His chest tightened, breath coming in shallow gasps. Leon, his closest friend, his confidant—was this how it would end? Was this how he would lose him?

The doctors called for a stretcher, and they loaded Leon on it. Still in his armor, it took several men to carry it.

Coriander followed behind, each step heavy with dread. The cheers of the crowd faded into a distant hum, overshadowed by the sound of his own racing thoughts. What if this was the end of the only true friendship he had? The tournament meant nothing now; all that mattered was seeing Leon alright again.

Chapter Fifteen

Coriander sat in a chair beside Leon's bed, his fingers interlaced with his friend's unmoving hand. Each moment felt like an eternity as he fought back the tears that threatened to spill over, knowing that once he was alone, there would be no stopping them. The room was oppressively quiet, save for the faint rustling of Leon's shallow breaths, each one a reminder of how fragile his life had become.

Hours had passed, but Leon remained unconscious, his chest rising and falling in shallow, uneven breaths. Each moment amplified Coriander's dread, the silence of the room growing heavier with every passing second. The doctors had done everything within their power, yet it wasn't enough. The wound might not have seemed severe, but the unknown loomed over them like a specter, its shadow growing longer with each passing hour.

Leon's head was now shaved, the ugly wound hidden beneath layers of bandages. But a small, ominous red spot slowly bloomed through the fabric, a stark contrast against the sterile whiteness. The doctors had reassured him that most head wounds looked worse than they were, but their words felt hollow in the stillness of the room. The real concern now was keeping Leon alive long enough to wake him from the sleep that bordered on death.

They had tried to coax him to swallow spiced water, but Leon had not responded, his body refusing the life-giving liquid. Without nourishment, without some miracle, the doctors had said, he would last no more than a few days—four or five at most, and that was if they were being optimistic.

Samuel entered quietly, the door creaking slightly as he slipped into the room. He set a tea tray on the table with a bowl of soup. "Try to eat, my lord. You need to keep up your strength as well."

"How?" Coriander's voice trembled, the sharpness of his unspilled tears lacing his words with bitterness. "How can I eat when he lies here like this?"

Samuel took a deep breath, steadying himself. "I do not mean to presume, sire, but I do not believe Sir Leon would approve of you behaving this way."

A half-caught sob escaped Coriander's lips. "Go away, Samuel," he choked out, the words harsh but tinged with the pain he could no longer contain.

Samuel bowed, his expression pained, though he knew better than to let the prince's sharp words wound him. He understood the depths of Coriander's grief and the strain it placed on him. As he turned to leave, he hesitated, then spoke softly.

"Apologies, sir. I was also instructed to inform you that the doctors found a few more things in the archives they would like to try. They should be up shortly."

Coriander didn't respond. His gaze remained fixed on Leon's still form, as if willing his friend to wake. Samuel cast a lingering glance at the prince, his heart heavy with concern, before quietly leaving the room.

Not much time had passed before the doctors returned, their faces lined with the weight of their task. They carried an array of vials and herbs, their hands moving with practiced precision. The scent of crushed lavender and bitter roots filled the air as they worked, relics of an ancient practice that now felt painfully inadequate. Coriander sat in silence, still holding Leon's hand, as they tried one remedy after another—tonics, creams, and procedures—all to no avail. Each failed attempt chipped away at Coriander's hope until one of the doctors finally spoke, his voice heavy with regret.

"I am sorry, Prince Coriander," he said. "We just don't know what else to try."

"You can't just give up!" Coriander's voice cracked with desperation as he rose, his hands trembling with the force of his emotions. The room seemed to close in around him, the walls echoing his plea.

"We aren't giving up," the man assured, though his tone betrayed his own hopelessness. "We will keep scouring the archives. But at this point, unless some magical cure is just lying around somewhere, we aren't sure what else to do."

Coriander's mind ground to a halt. Then, like a bolt of lightning, the thought struck him—magic. It was a wild, desperate hope, but it was something. Without another word, Coriander bolted from the room, the single word—magic—echoing in his mind, a lifeline in the darkness.

"Stop!" the gate guard shouted.

Coriander did not stop. Zedd burst between the two men, already at a full gallop, nearly bowling them over. His hooves rang against the cobblestones as Coriander urged him for more speed. Zedd gave all he could, but Coriander wasn't willing to run his friend to death, so he slowed their pace once they were beyond the city walls. Breathing hard and covered in a sheen of sweat, Zedd gave a soft neigh, as if thanking Coriander for the slower pace.

Once Coriander was sure they weren't being pursued, he slowed their pace even further, allowing Zedd to maintain a steady rhythm as they continued on their way. After all, he still had a day or two at worst.

The trip to the grotto seemed to take longer than usual, as the countryside slid by slowly. In most places, the damage from the storm was hardly noticeable anymore, though many areas were still undergoing rebuilding.

When he finally reached the ridge overlooking the forest, Coriander noticed the extensive work that had been done. A new, safer path had been carved into the ridge, making it easier for carts and horses to descend. The fallen trees had been cleared away, but the faint scent of freshly cut wood lingered in the air, a reminder of the storm's aftermath.

No one seemed to be around, so he urged Zedd down the ridge and onto the deer path. Remembering the state of the brook and pond when he'd last seen it, Coriander's heart filled with dread with each step Zedd took. It wasn't long before they arrived.

Coriander stood in stunned silence, unable to believe his eyes. The grotto had somehow been completely restored! The little brook trickled placidly down into the small pond again, and its edges were lined with reeds and scrub grass, just as they had been the first time he saw it. The water was clear and inviting, with no sign that it had ever overflowed its banks.

He tossed Zedd's lead over a low branch, within reach of both the water and a patch of grass. He gave the horse's head a loving scratch and promised to return soon. With his pack on his shoulder, he headed deeper into the woods.

After two hours of searching, Coriander was forced to give up. He was fairly sure he remembered the direction from the grotto, but despite his efforts, he could not locate the low cliff with the cave.

Shyne had told him that he would not find it again. Was it hidden now by some kind of fairy magic? Or had it ever really existed in the first place?

Defeated, he returned to the grotto. It was the last connection he had to Shyne. Zedd greeted him with a shake of his head, his eyes glinting with what Coriander could only describe as an 'I told you so' expression.

Not to be fully deterred, Coriander began Plan B. He laid out a thick, rich blanket he had brought along. Upon it, he set out several items: a large jar of honey, a couple of carafes of fresh milk, a bowl of mixed fruits, and a bottle of the best wine he could snag on short notice.

Zedd eyed the apples in the spread of fruit with jealousy, and Coriander couldn't help but indulge him. He fed one to the horse, receiving a soft, satisfied neigh in response.

He sat for a time, watching his precious day slip away. Nothing happened. Nothing changed. There was no sign of the fairy.

Growing frustrated, he stood and shouted into the woods.

"Shyne!" His cry seemed to be swallowed by the dense forest, dying out before it got anywhere.

"Shyne! Please, I need your help!" he tried again a few minutes later.

Letting a little more time pass, he called into the woods once more. "Please! My friend is hurt! If you can do anything to help him, I'll be forever indebted to you! Shyne!"

And then, there he was.

Shyne emerged from the bushes without a sound, as though he had been watching from the shadows all along. His bright green eyes blazed with fury, and his red hair flared like fire, dancing wildly with his every move. His wings folded into his back with an angry buzz.

"Thrice you have called," his normally soft voice dripped with disdain, "and thus I must answer. Be warned, Prince. All things come with a cost, so choose your next words carefully."

Coriander's heart pounded as the weight of his decision settled over him. He had promised to save Leon, but at what cost? Shyne's gaze bore into him, demanding compliance, yet it was the thought of his friend lying helpless that drove him to obey. There was no turning back now—he had made his choice.

"I will pay any price to save my friend," Coriander replied, his voice unwavering, betraying not a hint of doubt.

Shyne's wings buzzed to life, and in a blur of motion, he shot into the air, gliding over the blanket and its laden treats. He landed a few inches from Coriander, staring him in the eyes.

"I can get the medicine you need, but you will be mine, Prince Coriander. You will obey my every command without question. You will satisfy my every need. I will own your body, mind, and spirit until the autumn equinox passes. Do you accept these terms?"

For a brief moment, defiance flared in Coriander's chest. His instincts screamed to refuse, to fight back against this humiliating command. But as quickly as it arose, the thought was extinguished by the reminder of what was at stake. Swallowing his pride, Coriander began to undress, each movement weighted with resignation.

"Yes!" he answered, his voice carrying the weight of a hammered coffin nail.

Shyne grabbed him suddenly, his strength surprisingly immense for a man of such a small frame. Their lips pressed together in a long kiss. Shyne's lips tasted sweeter than any honey, and he smelled of spring. It was intoxicating, made even more so by the tingling energy spreading through Coriander's body from his lips. Once it had reached his fingertips and toes, Shyne broke the contact.

"The deal is made!" Shyne's voice rang out, echoing through the trees. His wings buzzed again as he shot into the air. He spun around, turned, and dove back toward the earth. He hit the surface of the pond, vanishing below the water with barely a ripple.

Coriander could do little more than stand there, shocked. Was this the right thing? Could he truly go through with this? It was too late for second thoughts, he knew. He could feel that fact deep in his spirit.

Moments later, the surface of the pond erupted as Shyne arose. He walked up the bank with water streaming down his body, something clenched between his fists. He opened them to reveal a bright green mushroom that seemed to almost give off its own light.

"Break off a piece of the cap large enough to fit under your friend's tongue. Leave it there, it will work its magic. Depending on how severe his mind has been damaged, it may take several hours. But he will awaken."

Coriander took the mushroom and began to stow it in his pack. He stopped suddenly and looked up at Shyne. "I never told you about Leon's injury."

The fairy gave a wicked grin. "I see more than you can imagine, my prince," he said with a knowing smile, the weight of his words hanging in the air.

The mushroom safely stowed in his bag, Coriander stored it away on Zedd's saddle. He was just raising his foot to the stirrup when Shyne's sharp "Stop!" made him freeze.

Literally, he could not move a muscle as that warm energy spread through his body once more.

"To me." Shyne commanded, indicating the ground in front of him. Coriander's body obeyed without his control. He stood before the fairy, his body quivering as his mind tried to fight the control.

"I prefer not to have an unwilling servant. But I wanted you to understand the power I have over you until the equinox. As long as you do as I say, I will not use this geas again to force you to obey." The warm feeling fled Coriander's body, and he found himself back in control. "Do you understand?"

"I do," he acknowledged with a nod of his head.

"Good. Now strip."

Coriander stood dumbfounded, staring at Shyne as if not comprehending. The fairy sighed.

"I do not like to repeat myself."

The warmth began to creep across Coriander's body again, but retreated when he quickly obeyed. He undid the buttons of his tunic and slid it off, revealing his tanned skin, and muscular arms and chest. Untying his trousers, they and his loincloth followed.

Shyne walked around him, his eyes sizing him up as if a fresh cut of meat. Coriander jumped as he felt the man's fingers run gently down his spine. His fingers traced invisible lines all across the prince's body, leaving indelible marks in his mind.

Hands grabbed and squeezed his buttocks, poked and prodded his muscles. Fingers traced circles around, and then gently pinched his nipples.

Coriander endured the teasing, compliant but unaroused. Finally, Shyne stood in front of him again, his wicked grin promising dark things. The fairy's hand wrapped around his manhood and began to gently stroke it. For once, Coriander did not rise to the occasion.

Shyne frowned, then sighed, his gaze softening slightly. "You are too worried for your friend." The statement was simple, bearing no accusation, only understanding. He stepped back, giving Coriander space. "As I said, I will not have an unwilling servant. Go to your friend, and give him the medicine. But, my prince," again with that heavy inflection on 'my,' "you will return to me three days hence."

A surge of relief washed over Coriander, and before he could stop himself, he embraced Shyne. The fairy stiffened for a moment, caught off guard, but then returned the hug gently, his slender fingers brushing lightly against Coriander's back.

"Thank you," Coriander whispered, the words full of sincerity. He broke the embrace, dressed, and mounted Zedd, departing without another word.

Shyne watched him ride away, a contemplative look in his bright green eyes. What trouble had he invited into his life by claiming the prince? He knew he couldn't truly force Coriander to do anything he didn't want to do—his kind didn't wield that sort of power over mortals. It may have felt that way to Coriander, but it had all been mere illusion, a few magical tricks that wouldn't work again.

He sighed deeply, the sound almost lost in the quiet of the forest. What would the future hold now? At least he had a plaything to entertain him for the time being, but something in Coriander's sincerity had unsettled him in a way he hadn't expected.

Shrugging to himself, Shyne sat on the fine blanket, examining the gifts the prince had left behind. The faint scent of honey and wine filled the air as he uncorked one of the carafes, his mind already drifting to the days ahead. No reason to let these offerings go to waste.

Chapter Sixteen

The hours dragged by, with no improvement in Leon's condition. The doctors had thought him mad when he presented them with the mushroom and explained how to use it—especially since he couldn't fully explain how he knew or where he had obtained it. But in the end, an order from the Prince was obeyed.

Coriander sat staring out the window, his gaze distant, as if he could see the grotto far away. His thoughts swirled, tangled with questions about what the fairy had in store for him.

The deadline of three days was now less than two days away. How was he even going to get out of the city again? He was certain the guards must have reported his earlier escape, and he assumed the only reason his father hadn't come down on him yet was due to Leon's condition.

"Pfffff-yuck. What tastes so bad?"

Coriander spun around. Leon was sitting up in bed, raking his fingernails across his tongue with a comical expression on his rough face, blinking as his eye adjusted to the strong daylight.

The prince hit him like a bolt, embracing him in a tight hug. "Leon!" he sobbed.

"Ack! Okay, okay." Leon awkwardly patted his back in return. After a moment of silence, he whispered, "Did I win?"

Coriander leaned back, surprised. "Win?"

"The joust?"

Coriander slapped his friend's shoulder. "No, you oaf. You were very severely knocked unconscious."

"Ah!" Leon breathed out. "That would explain why my head feels like a cracked egg then." He reached up to scratch at the bandages.

Coriander embraced him again. "Thankfully, you're going to be okay now."

"Must have been a pretty good knock to the head too. I had the strangest dream about fairies and mushrooms." Coriander's breath caught in his throat.

"What do you mean?" he asked, leaning in closer, his heart pounding as he met Leon's gaze.

"I don't really remember much, just..." Leon winced and reached up to rub the area around his eye patch. "Something isn't right." He muttered, pulling the patch off.

The sight took Coriander by such surprise that he couldn't stop his gasp of shock or the look of horror that crossed his face. His friend's once empty eye socket now held a bloodshot eye with a colorless iris. Even the old scar across the socket had faded to nearly nothing.

Leon held up his hands and closed his good eye, waving his fingers in front of the other. "I can see!" he exclaimed. "It's shapes and shadows at best, but Cory, I can see!"

By that afternoon, most of the red veins had vanished from the knight's new eye, and color had returned to the iris. His vision was also improving, now with everything appearing as colorful, blurry blobs.

The doctors were baffled and wanted to study the rest of the mushroom for the obvious miracle cure it was. But what remained of it had seemingly vanished from the jar they had stored it in.

So it was during this time of chaos that Coriander chose to pull a vanishing act as well. Dressed in the plainest clothing he could find and a dull, well-worn leather cloak, he managed to slip through the gates that evening before they were shut for the night.

Unable to bring Zedd for this trip, he had to pack lightly. Just a few provisions and other small items he might need. He traded his sword, something too easily recognized, for a couple of belt daggers and a small bow and quiver.

He walked most of the night. The main roads of the kingdom were usually safe enough. A few hours before dawn, he finally stopped at a small inn to get a little sleep. He wasn't going to be missed at the castle until midday at the earliest. Even with horses, he already had an impressive lead on them and would reach the grotto long before they even set out to search.

He ate a light breakfast, provided by the inn, and set out again just after dawn. The way took much longer on foot than it had on horseback, but he still managed to get there just after noon.

As Coriander approached the grotto, the air seemed to hum with a quiet energy, the scent of damp earth and wildflowers mingling with something sweeter—something otherworldly. The sunlight filtered through the leaves, casting dappled shadows that danced on the ground, as if the forest itself were alive, watching, waiting.

Shyne looked up at him with a mischievous grin. "Even with a few hours to spare. Very well done, my prince." He was sitting in the pond, submerged to just below his nipples. As he rose from the water, he gestured to the blanket Coriander had left on his last visit. "Sit," he commanded.

Coriander removed his bag, storing his belt daggers inside. He placed it and his bow among the rocks of the small cliff face. Then he did as instructed and sat down on the blanket.

The gifts he had left were gone, replaced by strange, covered dishes and a large golden ewer. The pitcher's spout was adorned with a king's ransom worth of rubies, each gem catching the light with a fiery glint.

Across the blanket from him, Shyne sat down as well. He indicated the spread of covered dinnerware set between them. "You have brought me gifts of exquisite tastes from your land. Now allow me to repay you in kind. Let it not be said that I am not a proper host." He lifted the cover off one of the dishes. Underneath sat what appeared to be a small pastry. The base was a golden yellow cake with a layer of frosting on top, the colors swirling into an intricate, mesmerizing design.

"This one is Cool Breeze on a Warm Day." Shyne smiled, offering him the pastry. "Try it."

Coriander took a small, cautious bite. He didn't even have the words to describe the flavor. Sweet was inadequate. Wonderous fell flat. Orgasmic wasn't even close. But even more shocking than the flavor were the sensations it caused. He felt the warm sun on his skin, the light cool breeze that wicked away the non-existent sweat from his skin.

Shyne grinned widely, his eyes gleaming with satisfaction as Coriander gasped in sudden elation. "Now you have a taste of what it's like for the fair-folk. Our food isn't just taste, but sensation. Concepts made whole to whet not just the appetite, but to satisfy the mind."

Just Before the Thunderstorm was next. With a bite, Coriander experienced the smell of coming rain, the strengthening breeze that brought with it a few cold, stinging droplets. The feel of lighting in the air, and the distant crash of thunder. He looked up at the clear, blue sky, struggling to reconcile the stark contrast between what he felt and what he saw. The sensations were so real, his mind teetered on the edge of disbelief. Was this what it was like to go mad?

For a brief moment, a flicker of doubt crossed Coriander's mind. Was this all too easy? Too perfect? But Shyne's eyes gleamed with such promise, such allure, that the doubt was quickly swallowed by the anticipation building within him.

As the sensations finally loosened their grip on him, Coriander became acutely aware of Shyne beside him, the fairy's lips brushing against his neck as nimble fingers expertly undid the buttons of his tunic.

"Do you consent to me, my prince?" Shyne whispered into Coriander's ear, the words sweet with the promise of what was to follow.

Coriander's heart raced, not just from the sensations, but from the implications of what he was about to do. Was this real desire, or simply a yearning for something—anything—that could fill the void inside him? The fairy's touch was intoxicating, but the doubt lingered, a shadow at the edges of his mind. "Yes," Coriander responded breathlessly.

Shyne's smile broadened. "One last thing then. We will save the other treats for later, but this," he lifted the pitcher, "will make this experience one your mortal mind shall never forget."

He lifted the spout to the prince's lips. Reflexively, Coriander began to drink deeply. After the sweets, he thought surely nothing could ever surpass such flavor. He was wrong. It warmed him from the inside with a pleasant tingle to every corner of his body. Lightning coursed through every muscle, and fire burned through his spirit.

"This is Fairy Nectar," he heard Shyne whisper to him as he drank.

He lay naked on the blanket, unable to recall when his clothes had been removed. The crisp crystal blue of the sky above overwhelmed his senses, bringing tears to his eyes. Around him, the breath of the ancient trees whispered, a lazy rush of air from beings that had stood on this land longer than most creatures had walked it. Beneath him, he could feel the earthworms tunneling through the soil, their movements a subtle vibration in the ground. The cry of a nearby raven was a symphony in his ears, every sound heightened, every sensation magnified.

But above all else, his body reported an undeniable truth. He was hard, his cock standing up as if it too were reaching for the sky.

Shyne's kisses felt like planted seeds, blooming into beautiful flowers of sensation as his lips moved from one spot to the next. He kissed slowly down Coriander's neck, crossing over to his chest. His fingers roamed over the prince's muscles, each touch a whirlwind of pleasure.

A moan slipped from Coriander's lips, nearly animalistic and full of desire.
Shyne's tongue flicked across the prince's stiffened nipple, sending lightning through his veins. Coriander

nearly lost himself right then and there, his back arching, his cock throbbing toward release.

"Not yet," Shyne whispered, and the feeling slowly subsided. His kisses continued down to Coriander's stomach. Coriander grasped the blanket in his hands with a loud cry of pleasure as the fairy's chin brushed the sensitive head of his erect member. Shyne chuckled at the reaction, teasing the underside of the tip with his tongue. Lightning shot to Coriander's fingers and toes, and again his body pushed toward climax.

"Not yet." This time it was a command, stern and unforgiving. Coriander's body bucked against it, but the sensation once again subsided.

Shyne positioned himself between Coriander's legs, his fingers dipping into the pitcher of Fairy Nectar. He rubbed the liquid onto his own erect cock, the fiery bush at its base shimmering as his member grew longer and thicker.

Coriander's breath caught in his throat, the anticipation coiling tightly within him. Time seemed to stretch, each moment a breathless eternity as he waited for the connection he both craved and feared. The wet tip of Shyne's cock pressed against Coriander's entrance as he leaned forward. Coriander moaned in anticipation. Shyne grinned down at him. "Ready?"

Coriander could do nothing more than nod. Shyne leaned down to him and locked their lips into a deep kiss. Simultaneously, his cock pushed into Coriander's hole. A brief, dull pain accompanied the initial penetration, but it quickly dissolved as the Nectar spread warmth through his core.

Shyne slowly slid his full length into Coriander, never breaking their deep kiss. Coriander's breath quickened, his moans vibrating against Shyne's lips. His legs hooked onto the fairy's thighs, and his hands reached up to stroke Shyne's back. His fingers brushed against something soft, silk-like—a realization cutting through the haze of ecstasy that Shyne's wings were unfurled.

Shyne's wings beat softly in time with his thrusts, their delicate, gossamer edges catching the light and shimmering like silk. His lips continued to explore Coriander as they writhed together on the blanket.

Their hands explored, their lips pressed together, creating a symphony of moans that filled the air. Each movement was deliberate, precise, designed to draw out the greatest sensations from their entwined bodies.

Shyne's thrusts grew steadily faster, each movement calculated to heighten the intensity. Coriander became lost in the rhythm, his senses overwhelmed as the world around him seemed to blur. The sky above them morphed with dizzying speed—day bled into night, the stars spun in constellations he didn't recognize, and the sun chased the moon in a fevered dance. Colors he couldn't name painted the horizon, each shade pulling him deeper into Shyne's embrace, blurring the line between reality and dream.

Every touch from Shyne was a double-edged sword—pleasure laced with the sharp sting of uncertainty. Was this what he wanted, or was he surrendering to something beyond his control? The intensity of it all frightened him, but it also drew him in, like a moth to a flame, knowing the burn but needing the light.

Shyne's lips lingered against Coriander's skin, but there was a fleeting hesitation in his touch—a barely perceptible pause that hinted at something more beneath his wicked smile. Was he enjoying this as much as Coriander, or was there another purpose to his every move?

Coriander's body tensed, every nerve on fire as Shyne's rhythm pushed him closer to the edge. The world around him seemed to hold its breath, the sky pausing in its frantic dance, as if even time itself waited for the moment of release. And then, all at once, the dam broke, and Coriander was lost in a flood of sensation that drowned out everything else.

Coriander's release surged between their bodies, each wave of climax intensifying the shuddering ecstasy that pulsed through him. His back arched, and every muscle shook. His fingers dug into Shyne's back as if trying to merge them both into one body.

Shyne had stopped his thrusts. He was breathing quickly but softly in Coriander's ear. The prince's own breaths were ragged and shaky. Shyne pulled free of him and laid down beside him, kissing Coriander's neck softly.

"Rest a moment, for I have not had my full pleasure yet." The whisper was barely a breath in Coriander's ear.

Coriander stared up at the clear blue sky above, his body aching with exhaustion, yet desire still coiled within him. The notion that this was only the beginning filled him with both anticipation and a flicker of fear. How much more could he endure, and how much more did he want to?

"How…" his voice was still trembling, and sounded miles away, "how many days was that?"

Shyne smiled that wicked and mischievous smile of his, a fleeting glint of something unreadable in his eyes. "Oh my dear prince," he whispered, his voice a tantalizing promise of what was still to come. "That was only the first hour."

Coriander's body trembled with fatigue, but his mind raced. Shyne's words echoed in his ears—a promise, a warning, or perhaps both. As he lay there, still trying to catch his breath, a part of him wondered if he had the strength to endure what was to come. But another part, the part that was still entwined with Shyne, was ready to surrender completely.

Chapter Seventeen

With a grunt and a low moan, Shyne finally released into Coriander. The prince felt the warmth of it but reacted only by leaning his head back against the fairy's shoulder. They sat together, partially submerged in the pond. Evening had set in, and the sky was beginning to darken.

He had spent hours now in the grasp of the fairy's lovemaking. Each time he thought it could go on no longer, another bite of the Fey food or a sip of Nectar would restore his strength, and they would be at it again.

Now he lay against Shyne's heaving chest, barely breathing as bone-deep exhaustion settled over him. Despite the weariness, his mind buzzed with a confusing mix of emotions—desire, longing, and a growing sense of unease.

"Wonderful, my prince," Shyne whispered in his ear, the touch of his breath sending shivers down Coriander's spine. Something soft pressed against the prince's lips. "One last bite. You'll need your strength for the walk home."

Coriander accepted the treat, which melted in his mouth almost instantly. Warmth spread through his body as his vision blurred. Suddenly, he had the sensation of soaring through the air, high up on a warm updraft with his feathered wings spread wide. His sharp eyes caught a slight movement on the ground below. He dove, the wind blasting around him. His talons raked forward just as a mouse scurried from the bushes...

They kissed again, but this time it was not the passionate kiss that had preceded their lovemaking. This was a kiss of farewell, spiced with future promises.

"Three days," Shyne growled heavily, "and you will return to me."

Coriander's heart ached as they parted, the weight of Shyne's final kiss lingering on his lips. He felt a confusing mix of longing and weariness, as if he were being pulled in two directions at once—toward the fairy's irresistible allure and the reality of the life he had to return to. A pang of guilt twisted in his chest as he thought of Leon. What would Leon think if he knew where Coriander had been, who he had been with? The fairy's allure was impossible to resist, but with each encounter, Coriander felt a growing distance between himself and the life he had known. Was he losing himself in the fairy's world, or was this where he truly belonged?

At first, all he could manage was a nod, but already he was feeling the restorative energy of the fairy treat flooding his body. Finally, he groaned out a weak "Yes."

They eventually separated and rose from the waters, the cool evening air wrapping around Coriander like a soothing balm, cooling his flushed skin. The pond was still, its surface reflecting the darkening sky like a mirror. The trees around them loomed tall and silent, their leaves rustling softly in the evening breeze. The air smelled of damp earth and moss, grounding Coriander in the present even as his mind swirled with the remnants of the fairy's magic. He stumbled a bit as he made his way out of the pond, his legs becoming stronger and more steady with each step. The sounds of the night—crickets chirping, leaves rustling—seemed more vivid now, pulling him back to reality as he dressed quickly, gathered his things, and prepared to leave.

As Coriander dressed, he noticed how his hands trembled slightly, still weak from the hours of intense passion. The evening light had faded to dusk, casting long shadows on the ground. Each movement felt deliberate, as if he were trying to prolong his time in this otherworldly place, even though he knew he had to go.

Shyne stopped him, planting a final soft kiss on his lips. "Three days," he reminded the prince.

"Yes," Coriander repeated his agreement, his voice stronger and steadier now. Shyne smiled that wicked grin, but Coriander couldn't shake the feeling that there was something more behind it—something calculated, as if every touch, every word, had been carefully orchestrated. Was he truly a willing participant in this dance, or was he being led by forces he didn't fully understand?

As Coriander pulled on the last of his clothing, he couldn't help but feel a lingering sense of disorientation. The fairy's touch was as light as a whisper, his breath a gentle breeze against Coriander's ear. The fairy's presence felt both comforting and dangerous, like the pull of a tide that could either carry you to safety or drag you under.

The treat had melted on Coriander's tongue like spun sugar, filling his senses with a warmth that spread through his veins. His vision had blurred for a moment, and suddenly he was soaring through the air, the ground a distant memory beneath his wings. The sensation was exhilarating, almost intoxicating, as if the very essence of the fairy's world had seeped into his soul.

As he finally turned to leave, the weight of the past hours settled on Coriander's shoulders, heavy and undeniable. The memory of Shyne's touch and the lingering taste of the fairy's kiss filled him with a longing that was both thrilling and unsettling. Each step away from the pond felt like a betrayal of something sacred, but the pull of his other life—of duty and obligation—was just as strong. He knew he would return in three days, but what would he find waiting for him when he did? And what part of himself would he leave behind this time?

He could only hope he was ready for it.

On the journey back, he spent the night at the same inn, collapsing into a dreamless sleep. His body and mind were too drained to conjure anything more than the emptiness of rest. After all, how could any dream compare to the events of the last day?

He descended the creaky stairs of the old inn early the next morning, only to find Leon waiting for him at a corner table. The knight's stern glare cut through the morning haze, his eyes locking onto Coriander as he silently gestured to the chair across from him.

Coriander slumped into the chair, his head bowed in resignation. The silence between them was thick, broken only by the soft clink of a tea tray as the serving girl placed it on the table. "Food will be out shortly," she murmured with a smile, before quickly disappearing into the kitchen.

Leon sighed, his frustration palpable. "Thankfully, I convinced your father not to send out an entire brigade to search for you. I told him I knew where you go when you need to be alone—and that I could bring you back safely."

Coriander gave his friend an appreciative look. It really was amazing how different Leon looked now. If not for the bit of missing eyebrow where the scar was, you would never have known he'd had the injury. The eye looked perfectly normal and natural, just like its twin.

"How's your vision?" Coriander asked, trying to shift the conversation as he poured himself a cup of tea.

"Perfect. Maybe even better than the good eye." Leon blinked and then crooked a small smile. "Well, I guess they're both the good eye now."

"Imagine that," Coriander murmured, taking a sip of his tea.

Leon's smile faded as he leaned forward, his expression growing serious. "Yeah, we're going to have a talk about that at some point. You escape the city like you had hell on your heels, then return with some magic mushroom?"

"Not really much of a story," Coriander shrugged, hoping to deflect.

"Bullshit." Leon's hands gripped the sides of the table as he leaned in closer. "Is this...person you're meeting with dangerous? I don't want you getting hurt."

Coriander noticed the way Leon emphasized the word "person," his tone a mix of concern and accusation. Was it the magic that troubled Leon, or something else?

Coriander looked away, caught between the urge to confess and the need to protect his secret. This was Leon—his best friend since childhood. Surely, he of all people would understand. But before Coriander could answer, the arrival of the food saved him.

Leon had ordered a feast for both of them, the tray piled high with eggs, bacon, sausage, and fresh bread. The smell was comforting, rich with the promise of a hearty meal, but as Coriander took his first bite, the flavors seemed muted—dull compared to the vibrant tastes of the fairy food.

He ate anyway, like a man starving, and felt some of his vitality begin to return. Leon joined him, more reserved, and they spent the next few minutes eating in silence.

Stopping by the stables on their way out, Coriander was greeted by an eager whinny from Zedd. The familiar sound brought a faint smile to his lips. He took his time patting the horse down, his fingers trailing through the coarse mane, before saddling him with practiced care.

With Leon on Gemstone, they set out back to the capital. Silence settled between them, leaving Coriander alone with his thoughts. His mind drifted back to the events of the previous day, the memories replaying themselves over and over. Each time, he felt a flush rise to his cheeks, forcing him to shift uncomfortably in the saddle.

His thoughts churned with guilt and confusion. The allure of the fairy was undeniable, yet it terrified him. What was he getting himself into? And then there was Samuel—how could he keep using the young man for comfort when his heart was so tangled up in something else?

"What are you going to tell your father?" Leon asked as the city came into sight.

"That I was repaying a debt."

His father was not pleased with the explanation. The next time Coriander left his room, he was met with an unexpected sight—guards stationed at the end of the hall. To his knowledge, there had never been guards within the royal quarters before. The sight sent a chill down his spine, a silent reminder of his father's displeasure.

He tried to dismiss them, but they remained steadfast, explaining with polite firmness that they were under strict orders from the king to stay by his side or escort him wherever he needed to go. The refusal only deepened Coriander's frustration, his anger simmering beneath the surface.

The walls of the castle, though grand and imposing, felt like a gilded cage, the heavy silence broken only by the echo of his footsteps. Each time Coriander ventured out of his chambers, he felt the eyes of the guards on him, a constant reminder of his father's iron grip. A confrontation with the king was inevitable, and the thought sent a shiver of dread down his spine.

How was he going to escape again before the fairy's deadline? What if he failed to make it in time? Would Shyne take back the gifts he'd given? Could he even do that? And if he did, what would it mean for Leon?

The questions gnawed at him, a constant reminder of the tangled web he was caught in. Coriander paced back and forth in his chambers, certain he was going to wear a rut in the rug. He had a little less than two days to figure something out.

A knock at the door interrupted his thoughts.

"Go away," the prince ordered darkly. The door pushed open anyway.

"Apologies, sire." It was the voice of Samuel. "You missed dinner, and I was ordered to bring you a tray."

"Samuel." Some of the anger bled from Coriander's voice. He helped the chamberlain settle the large silver tray onto the small table in the sitting area. Coriander eyed the spread. He was, of course, hungry, but everything still tasted so plain to him now.

"Join me," he requested of the young servant. "I know you haven't eaten yet. Not properly anyway."

"I can't, I have..."

"Samuel," the prince looked at him pointedly, "have I let you get in trouble yet?"

"No, my lord."

"And stop that while you're in my chambers. Call me Cory, or Coriander if that's too informal."

Samuel hesitated, a nervousness passing across his face. Such an act of improper protocol was nearly heresy among the staff. Coriander could see the struggle in the chamberlain's eyes.

"Or not, whatever you're comfortable with."

"Yes, my lord." Samuel sat at the table, and they ate together. Mostly they chatted about castle gossip. The staff always knew the best rumors.

They spent the evening trading stories and laughter, the warmth between them growing with each shared word. Eventually, Coriander brought out a bottle of wine, and as the night deepened, so did their connection. One glass led to another, and before long, the space between them vanished, leaving nothing but the heat of their shared breath and the gentle brush of their hands as they drew closer, until they found themselves in each other's arms.

Chapter Eighteen

He pulled Samuel down on top of him, a gentle descent to the bed while their lips were locked in passion. Their hands roamed across each other's bodies, removing clothes wherever they could, savoring the closeness.

The young servant carried the scent of the kitchens with him—a blend of warm spices, sweet confections, and the faint hint of wood smoke that clung to his skin. As Samuel's lips and tongue began to explore his body, the prince softly moaned, the sensation awakening something deep within him.

After his time with Shyne, Coriander hadn't thought that anything could ever measure up to the experience. But Samuel's gentle kissing and teasing touches stirred nearly the same fire and need within him that the fairy's had. A nagging thought surfaced in Coriander's mind—was this real, or was he simply trying to recapture the intensity he had felt with Shyne? The doubt flickered like a dying ember, but he pushed it aside, focusing instead on the warmth of Samuel's touch, the comfort of another's presence.

Samuel's lips trailed a warm path up Coriander's chest, each kiss like a brush of silk igniting a new spark of desire. When their lips met again, their now-naked bodies pressed fully together, their hard cocks sliding against each other, their movements synchronized in a dance of growing need.

The chamberlain's lips brushed ever so slightly across the prince's cheek, and then he softly bit Coriander's neck. The light pain caused him to gasp in surprise, which quickly was overrun with desire at the sensation. Samuel chuckled at the mixed reaction.

"Is that what you like, my prince?" Shyne whispered in his ear. Not Shyne, Coriander reminded himself, shaking his head slightly to clear the confusion. It was Samuel—kind, gentle Samuel—who was with him now, and yet the memory of the fairy's touch still lingered like a ghost in the back of his mind.

Coriander looked up at Samuel and saw the gleaming desire there. He locked eyes with Samuel, his gaze heavy with unspoken longing. With a deliberate move, he conveyed his offer, a silent invitation that sent a shiver of anticipation through the air between them. Samuel didn't hesitate, licking and kissing along the length of the prince's shaft. Coriander groaned as Samuel's tongue reached the tip, and his warm, wet mouth enveloped it.

Their breathing quickened, and Coriander moved his hips slightly to complement Samuel's rhythm. One hand reached back to stroke the servant's erect member.

Samuel twitched hard at the touch, a surprised gasp escaping even as muffled as it was. For a brief moment, they paused, their breath mingling in the space between them. The world outside seemed to fade away, leaving only the sound of their quickened breathing and the soft crackle of the fire. Coriander felt the tension coiling inside him, a taut string waiting to snap, as he leaned in closer, bridging the gap between them with a kiss that was both a question and an answer.

They moved together and moaned together. Feeling like he was reaching the breaking point, Coriander slid back from Samuel, a momentary look of disappointment crossing the servant's face. Noticing the flicker of doubt in Samuel's eyes, Coriander hesitated for a brief moment, then gently guided Samuel's length between his buttocks. He leaned down, brushing his lips against Samuel's ear in a reassuring whisper.

"I want you inside me."

Samuel's eyes went wide, a flicker of fear—or was it hesitation?—flashing across his face. For a moment, the confidence he had shown seemed to waver, replaced by uncertainty as he looked up at Coriander, searching for reassurance.

Seeing the uncertainty in Samuel's eyes, Coriander softened, cupping the man's cheek with a tender hand. "Only if you want to," he added, his voice gentle and steady. The fear deepened in the man's eyes.

"No...no...no!" he stammered. His hips bucked, and his hands pushed the prince off him. He sprang from the bed, gathering his clothes quickly and rushing for the door.

"Samuel!" the prince called, but Samuel didn't hesitate; he was already out the door, naked and clutching his clothes.

Coriander's heart sank as the door slammed shut. What had he done to drive Samuel away? Was it his fault for acting on impulse, or was something darker lurking beneath Samuel's reaction? Guilt gnawed at him, twisting his gut with the fear that he had only added to Samuel's pain.

After a moment, he sighed and pulled on his trousers, resolving to find Samuel and apologize—whatever he had done to upset him.

Padding to the door barefoot, Coriander made his way down the hall. The corridor was dimly lit, the flickering torchlight casting long, eerie shadows that seemed to stretch endlessly along the cold stone walls. The chill in the air seeped into Coriander's bones, heightening the sense of foreboding that had settled over him. He barely noticed until the last second that the guards were not there. Then he heard a sharp cry of pain from around the corner, followed by a gruff laugh.

"Ah, don't be gettin' shy now, boy. I know what you like," a deep, rough voice intoned.

Coriander stepped around the corner, and his blood ran cold at the sight before him. The air was thick with the acrid scent of sweat and fear, the stone walls amplifying the sounds of gruff laughter and muffled cries. One of the guards had Samuel pinned against the cold stone wall, his arm twisted cruelly behind his back. Samuel's clothes were strewn across the floor, and his eyes held a detached, hollow look, as if he had already resigned himself to the abuse.

The guard, trousers around his ankles, was pressing his erect cock against Samuel's ass in what he probably thought was a teasing manner. The other guard stood by, a horrified look on his face, completely unaware of the prince's approach.

Coriander's fist smashed into the back of the guard's head with the force of a hammer, sending him crashing forward into the stone wall, his forehead striking with a sickening thud. The guard stumbled back, dazed but still a trained soldier, and swung to meet the attack. Coriander, however, often trained with the kingdom's battle-hardened knights.

Ducking under the wild swing, Coriander drove his next blow into the soft spot just below the guard's breastbone. All the air whooshed out of the man's lungs as he doubled over. Grabbing the man's head as he stooped, Coriander slammed it into his raised knee. The guard's nose crunched under the impact, and with a breathless cry of pain, he fell to the ground on his back.

Blood streamed between the guard's fingers as he grasped his broken nose, and finally dragging in a gasping breath, he began to wail in pain.

"In this house, we do not harm the innocent," Coriander said, the quiet anger in his voice seeming to shake the walls of the corridor with its withheld fury. He stepped down on the guard's trousers as he attempted to back away. The material was still caught around his ankles, stopping his retreat.

"And we most certainly do not do what you just attempted to anybody." Coriander's other foot came down less than gently on the guard's genitals.

The man wailed in shocked pain. Coriander bore down his weight for a moment, until the guard's wail began to die from his lack of breath. The guard struggled to suck in more air, but the pain wouldn't let him. Finally, after a few moments of agony, the prince took his weight off his foot.

"Is that understood?" Barely a whisper, the question cut the air like a knife. The guard sucked in a deep breath, unable to answer verbally but shook his head in the affirmative as gracefully as his broken nose would allow.

Coriander stepped back, releasing the man's trousers. He pointed at the other guard. "Arrest him. Seven days in the stockades—no food, half water. Then banish him."

Coriander turned his fiery gaze to the other guard. "And don't think for a moment you are off the hook for allowing this to happen."

The guard audibly gulped but came to attention with a salute. "Yes, sire!"

Coriander glanced around, his heart pounding from the adrenaline. But as the dust settled, he realized that Samuel was gone—along with his scattered clothes. The realization left a hollow ache in Coriander's chest; he had wanted to protect Samuel, but it seemed he had only driven him further away.

Sighing to himself, Coriander resigned to work on that situation later. For now, he went to find the Guard Captain to explain what had just happened and to make sure his wishes were known. As he made his way to the Guard Captain's quarters, Coriander's steps were heavy with the burden of what had just transpired. He knew this was only the beginning—there were deeper wounds that needed healing, and it would take more than orders and punishment to set things right.

Chapter Nineteen

Days passed, and Coriander grew more anxious with each passing moment. Yet, despite his mounting fear, he hadn't suffered any ill effects from the fairy's magic. Every time he left the royal quarters, a guard would shadow his every move, making it impossible to slip away unnoticed.

He hadn't seen Samuel in several days, and the rotating servants informed him that the chamberlain was feeling unwell and had been restricted to light duty for the time being.

The offending guard had completed his week in the stockades and was unceremoniously banished from the kingdom. Coriander's thoughts were a tangled mess of guilt and resentment. He wondered if the guard's punishment had been too harsh, but then the memory of Samuel's hollow eyes would resurface, and he'd decide it hadn't been harsh enough. He turned from the window, preparing to resume his nervous pacing—only to nearly scream in shock.

Shyne was seated at the tea table, his presence as startling as a thunderclap in the still night. He was pouring himself a cup of tea from a teapot that had long since gone cold. He added a sugar cube, gave it a quick stir, and took a sip. An offended expression crossed his face as he set the cup back down with a sharp clink of china.

"You have broken our contract," he said, his voice dripping with venom. One perfect eyebrow arched as he turned just enough to pierce Coriander with a glare that froze him in place.

"I can explain..." Coriander's voice was a weak whisper, but Shyne wasn't interested in excuses.

In one swift motion, Shyne leapt to his feet, the chair toppling and clattering to the floor behind him. "There is no explanation sufficient enough!" The quiet fury in his voice cut through Coriander like a blade. "At sunrise, prince"—Coriander noticed with a jolt that Shyne had dropped the usual 'my'—"your punishment will begin."

Without another word, Shyne shrank down to a small size, his wings spreading wide as he shot out the window. Nimbus red energy surrounded his body, and he streaked away like a fiery comet into the night.

Coriander just stood there, lost for words, fear churning in his stomach and a cold sweat breaking out along his skin.

He had hardly slept before the blaring sound of trumpets jolted him awake. He slipped loosely into some clothes and padded barefoot over to the window, his heart racing.

From his room, he had a fairly decent view of the main gates above the city. It was difficult to make out anything definitive from this distance, especially in the poor light of the sunrise, but he could see a large group of people dressed in brilliant colors marching through the streets. They carried flags and banners and were surrounding several figures riding strange horses.

The trumpets blasted again—the fanfare to announce arriving dignitaries.

Coriander rushed to fix his clothing, slid on his boots, and hurried from the room, his heart pounding with a mix of fear and urgency. The two guards took up positions behind him as he passed, but he barely noticed them. The corridors of the castle seemed to stretch on endlessly as he made his way to the throne room, each turn adding to the knot of anxiety tightening in his chest.

When he finally arrived, the trumpets blared once more, and the doors swung open to reveal the figure of a man. The man wore bright blue silken clothing with a turban on his head. He entered and announced, "It brings me great pleasure to announce Sultan Malik Al-Hakim of Zahra!"

"Enter and be welcome." Coriander's father boomed from the throne in his deep baritone. He was regally dressed in his finest red and gold attire, with his shining golden crown upon his head.

It almost always shocked Coriander to see his father. The years had not been kind to the king. His face was worn and wrinkled, and his once golden hair had faded to a grayish white. Coriander wondered if he saw his future in his father's face, a man barely more than twice his age.

The man who entered was a stark contrast. He was young and vibrant, with brown skin and dark hair poking out from under the bright white turban. The head covering was adorned with small glittering gems, and chains of gold and silver hung with tiny bells that chimed a merry chorus as he walked. The silk robes he wore were of sharp pastel colors, tastefully layered atop one another.

As he stopped at the base of the throne's dais, his two guards came to attention behind him as he bowed deeply to the king with a jiggling flourish.

"King Erik," the Sultan greeted, his voice heavily accented but clear. "My apologies for our tardiness. My father received your missive about the offer of open marriage to the prince, but was unable to attend due to failing health."

"The journey here was long and arduous, and fraught with dangers!" he continued dramatically, the tinkling of his bells punctuating his statements. "Sadly, the princess also could not attend, as she is caring for our father. But!" He bowed deeply again. "With your Majesty's understanding, I am fully authorized to negotiate in their absence."

The king mulled over these facts for a few moments. "I have not made a full decision yet on who shall marry the prince, so I will entertain your proposal...late as it may be." His tone seemed to suggest it had no chance of success, but decorum bid him to at least hear the Sultan out. "Come! Breakfast has been prepared, and I invite you to join. My servants will see to yours, and prepare your accommodations."

"Very very good!" the Sultan agreed. He turned towards Coriander, who up until now had been quietly observing. "I know business will come later, but for now, will the prince be joining us?"

The king turned, seeing Coriander for the first time. "Of course," he replied.

The breakfast table was laden with a feast of vibrant colors and rich aromas. The Sultan dug into the dish before him with a gusto that sent the scent of spiced meats and honeyed fruits wafting through the air. The sound of silverware clinking against porcelain mingled with the low murmur of conversation, and the flickering candlelight cast a warm glow over the room. But for Coriander, every bite tasted like ash, his mind too preoccupied to appreciate the flavors.

"Oh, a delicacy indeed!" the Sultan praised, digging into the dish in front of him ravenously. "You will have to let my servants prepare tomorrow's dinner, so you can experience a meal from my homeland!"

"I see no issues with that." The king swirled his wine in the silver goblet before taking a sip.

"It's good to get a taste of the world!" The Sultan speared a piece of meat on his fork and pointed it at Coriander. "Your son there, for instance, seems the kind of man to enjoy tastes from far-off lands."

Coriander nearly dropped his fork, but recovered quickly and continued eating.

"How so?" the king questioned.

"Ah, such is the way of the youthful, I find. You can see the sparkle of that desire in his eyes." The Sultan then winked at the prince with the eye his father couldn't see. For a moment, it shone green before the color changed back to simple brown.

Coriander stood with a cough, his fork clattering against the plate. "Please excuse me, Sultan. Father." With a bow to each man, he swept from the table and retreated to his room, his heart pounding with a mix of dread and anticipation.

Several hours later, in the dead of night, he came. Coriander's door creaked open without announcement, and standing in the shadows was the Sultan. As he stepped forward into the light, that visage melted away to reveal the nude and aroused form of Shyne.

"Ready for your punishment?" He smiled his wicked smile at the prince.

Chapter Twenty

Samuel paced up and down the corridor. He couldn't hide forever... couldn't keep running from his duties. Really, it hadn't been the prince's fault. He just couldn't even think about that... act... without panicking.

He shivered as if the temperature in the corridor had suddenly dropped. Sure, the man responsible had been dealt with, but that didn't stop the memories from haunting him... or the fear that clung to him like a second skin.

The corridor spun for a moment, and Samuel grabbed the wall to steady himself. His heart pounded so violently he thought it might burst from his chest. Each breath felt like a struggle, the air too thick, too heavy to draw in. A few deep breaths kept him from losing the little breakfast he'd managed to eat. He nearly bolted back to the servants' quarters right then and there.

Why couldn't he just let it go? The prince had dealt with the man—punished him severely. But even knowing that, Samuel couldn't banish the fear that clawed at his insides, couldn't stop the memories from tearing him apart.

Samuel gathered his willpower, forced his body to stop shaking, and continued forward. The cold stone walls loomed around him, their rough texture catching the flickering light of the torches that lined the corridor. The flames cast long, dancing shadows that seemed to reach out toward him, adding to the sense that the darkness itself was alive, feeding off his fear.

The next turn of the corridor brought him in sight of the royal quarters.

The guard smirked as Samuel approached, grasped his crotch through his trousers, and sneered, "Ready for more, boy?"

Samuel closed his eyes and shook his head. His own imagination was torturing him now. That guard was gone; he had nothing to fear from him anymore.

When his eyes opened again, the vision of the guard was gone. In fact, there was no one at all.

He looked around. No guards were there at all. Had the king rescinded his order?

Samuel's feet felt like lead as he forced himself down the corridor. Every step was a battle against the urge to flee, to return to the safety of the servants' quarters where his fear couldn't reach him.

The small window at the end of the corridor began to let in the pale light of dawn, casting long shadows across the stone floor. Samuel stared at the handle of the prince's door, his hand trembling as it hovered above the latch. Could he really go in? Would the prince see the terror etched in his face, feel the tremors in his touch? He took a shuddering breath, willing his body to obey.

He had heard from the other servants, the ones filling in for him, that the prince had asked after his health several times. He knew the prince wasn't angry with him, just concerned. The prince had even come to his rescue and punished the man responsible.

Still, he couldn't shake this fear.

The prince would still be sleeping. He could get in, take care of his morning duties, and be gone before the prince ever even woke. He had done it so many, many times.

He paused, heart pounding, the handle of the prince's door just within reach. He could still turn back... but he knew he couldn't keep running forever. His hand was on the latch, his body withered in place as his mind raced with a thousand fears. What if the prince was awake? What if the shadows of the past still lingered in the room, waiting for him? Samuel took one final breath, bracing himself for whatever awaited him beyond that door... and then, he pushed it open...

And froze.

As the door creaked open, the first thing Samuel noticed was the smell. The air was sweet and heavy with a blend of spices, undercut by the pungent odors of sweat and sex.

The prince lay on his stomach across the bed, his knees and arms splayed out. A man with fiery red hair was atop him, his hips moving in time with his labored breathing. The prince moaned weakly, blissfully, with each movement.

But none of that was even the strangest part. Huge, shimmering wings sprouted from the man's back, like those of a dragonfly. They beat the air with each stroke of his hips, like some counterbalance to his thrusts.

The prince's gaze was unfocused, his eyes glazed with passion. The stranger, however, was looking directly at Samuel. He smiled a huge smile, wicked, mischievous, and sweet all at once. His eyes gleamed a bright green as he raised one hand and crooked a 'come here' gesture at Samuel.

A primal force within him pulled Samuel forward, his feet moving as if under a spell. Without thinking, Samuel stepped into the room as the heavy door clicked shut behind him.

He froze just short of the bedside, where he could see the stranger's cock sliding in and out of the prince. A shudder of revulsion mixed with something darker rippled through him, as a buried memory clawed its way to the surface, screaming in his mind.

The bedding was soaked with sweat and other fluids, its blankets and coverings tossed in rumpled piles about the floor. On the nightstand sat a silver pitcher with rubies encrusted around its rim.

"Poor, broken Samuel." The stranger's fingers brushed against Samuel's cheek, sending jolts of sensation and desire coursing through his body. A soft moan escaped his lips. The scream deep inside him grew louder, but was still swallowed by the fog in his mind. The stranger's smile grew wider.

"He wants you, Samuel. Don't you, my prince?" The last two words came out in nearly a hiss.

"Samuel..." the prince moaned. His hand reached out and weakly grasped at the cloth of Samuel's trousers. He attempted to tug them down but didn't seem to have the strength to do so. Instead, he begged, "...please."

The prince's eyes were half-lidded, struggling to stay open. What little could be seen of his pupils were gaping black voids, barely encircled by a thin ring of blue. A dried, yellowish liquid crusted at the corners of his cracked lips, glittering faintly in the dim light.

"No..." Samuel whispered, somehow finding the will to take a step back. His grip too weak, the prince's hand slipped loose of his trousers. The scream inside him grew louder, harder to ignore now. "...not like this."

"Oh, you must get over this pathetic trauma," the stranger said, his voice pompous and arrogant now, tinged with anger. Then he began to change. His muscles bulged grotesquely beneath his skin, stretching it to the point of tearing. The red hair darkened, becoming a matted, oily black, while the once-bright eyes dulled to a predatory yellow. The wings that had once shimmered so beautifully shriveled and withered away, replaced by the hulking frame of a man Samuel had thought he'd never see again.

Samuel gasped, recognizing the figure that now stood before him—the guard from his nightmares. The scream inside him peaked.

"No... no... no!" Samuel repeated, retreating in a panic until his back slammed against the cold, unforgiving stone wall. The air in the room felt thick, oppressive, as though it carried the weight of unseen eyes. The flickering light from the few remaining embers cast strange, shifting shadows across the walls, making the entire chamber feel alive with malevolent intent. Something nearby rattled, and his hand instinctively grasped its handle.

"Come and take your turn, boy," the rough voice of the guard growled at him.

"No!" Samuel screamed, his voice now matching the one inside his head. His heart pounded in his chest, torn between the compulsion to obey the stranger's command and the revulsion churning in his gut. Why was this happening? Why was he powerless to resist, even as every fiber of his being screamed at him to run? Samuel's thoughts were a chaotic whirl, memories and fears colliding in a storm of confusion.

He raised the weapon, took two long strides forward, and swung. The guard raised his arm to block the sudden attack, and the weapon struck. A blinding flash of light erupted upon impact, and the guard vanished. The stranger screamed in horrid pain as he tumbled from the bed onto the floor.

The smell of burnt flesh overwhelmed the room, and Samuel saw the blackened streak across the stranger's forearm, its edges still cracked and smoking. The stranger cradled his arm to his chest as he slowly tried to crawl away.

"Whatever you've done to him isn't right," Samuel said, pointing to the prince as he stalked toward the stranger, still clutching the weapon in his hand. The prince lay there limply, breathing slowly and still moaning softly. "And it stops today. I don't care what you are—monster, demon—I'll kill you if you touch him again."

He pressed the tip of the weapon into the stranger's chest, realizing with the curved hook at the end that it was the fireplace poker. The stranger screamed in agony again, his skin blackening around the point of the poker.

The man shoved it away, receiving another burn to his hand in doing so. He scrambled as Samuel swung at him again, managing to dive out the open window before the chamberlain could land another blow.

Samuel ran to the window, expecting to see the man falling to his death. Instead, all he saw was a small red comet shooting off into the distance.

As the ball of red light vanished into the night sky, Samuel's heart sank with the uneasy certainty that this wasn't over. The sense of dread that had taken root in his soul refused to leave, whispering dark promises of what was still to come. He couldn't shake the feeling that the prince's torment—and his own—had only just begun.

He closed and locked the shutters, set the poker up against the nightstand, covered the prince as best he could, and began his duties.

Chapter Twenty-One

Coriander felt a warm, damp cloth press gently against his feverish forehead, the soothing touch briefly cutting through the fog of pain that clouded his mind. He moaned slightly at the sensation, but it wasn't a moan of pleasure; his head pounded like a drum. He started to crack open his eyes and instantly regretted it. As soon as the light touched them, his head pounded harder and his stomach churned.

"Uuurrrrpppp." He gurgled as his stomach revolted.

"Here, sire." A familiar voice spoke, and soft hands helped roll him onto his side just as everything started coming up. It sounded like it splashed into a nearby container, but all he could focus on was the smell—sickly sweet mixed with the foul scent of stomach acid.

It took a few minutes for everything to expel before he finally just lay there, dry heaving. Coughing and gasping for breath, he finally squeaked out a weak "Samuel?"

"I'm here, my lord." Samuel's voice was a soft whisper, which Coriander appreciated because even that volume made his head pound harder.

"Water…" he croaked. A moment later something touched his lips, and he felt the wetness on his tongue. He drank; the first few sips still had the taste of awful, but then that cleared away, leaving only cool and crisp water.

A couple more sips, and his stomach seized again, losing all the water a moment later. Samuel cooed reassurances as he held the bucket up to Coriander's lips. Once he was done, Samuel gave him a few smaller sips of water that seemed to stay down.

"Hot," Coriander complained, weakly trying to kick the heavy blanket off him. He felt Samuel's grip steady his legs, the normally thin man seeming to possess the strength of giants in that moment.

"No, sire," Samuel said, tucking the blanket back around him. "Your body is very cold; we have to keep you warm. You seem to have some kind of illness, but the castle doctor isn't sure what it could be."

Coriander risked opening his eyes again, and this time managed it slightly. He could see the blurry form of Samuel standing over him, wiping his forehead again with the warm cloth. He weakly raised one arm—it felt so heavy—and gently brushed Samuel's cheek.

"Samu…" was all he managed before a wave of exhaustion passed over him, and his vision went dark.

Samuel arranged the prince into a more comfortable position, then leaned down and placed a soft kiss on Coriander's forehead.

"I'm right here, Cory," he whispered, his voice trembling slightly with worry, as if he feared losing the prince to the darkness that had nearly consumed him.

The fever finally broke by the end of the day, but it took another full day before Coriander began to feel better. The castle doctor believed he must have been poisoned somehow. Considering the Sultan and his retinue had all mysteriously vanished that first night, the king was laying the blame on the desert kingdom. Whispers of possible war flew about the castle. Coriander's mind raced as he lay in bed, still feeling the phantom ache of the fever. How could he reconcile his duties as a prince with the turmoil in his heart? Shyne had saved him once, but at what cost? And now, with the threat of war looming, how could he ever trust his own judgment again?

When he finally felt up to it, he found himself sparring with Leon in the training yard, determined to shake off the lingering effects of his mysterious illness.

"Do you think it'll come to that?" Coriander asked, blocking a sword thrust. His breath came heavily but healthily.

"Who knows?" Leon grunted, attempting a sloppy riposte that Coriander blocked easily. Both men took a step back and began to circle one another, each probing the other's defense for a weakness.

"Your father sent knights out that morning to search for the fleeing party," Leon continued. Sweat dripped down his toned and tanned body, soaking into the waistband of his trousers. Coriander had to remind himself not to get distracted. Leon continued, "but they didn't find anything. The Sultan's group had a few hours' head start at least, but most were on foot. The mounted knights should have caught them quickly. There are only so many roads to the desert."

Coriander let his stance slip on purpose to bait Leon into an attack. Leon took the bait, and Coriander attempted a disarm maneuver. But Leon's attack had been a feint. He threw out a kick against the prince's knee. The blow landed, throwing off Coriander's balance and bringing him to the ground.

Before he could recover, the blunted blade of Leon's sword pressed to his neck. "Yield?" the knight asked.

"Never!" Coriander cried heroically, knocking Leon's sword away with his other hand and sweeping his own toward his friend's stomach while laughing.

Leon kicked the sword from the prince's hand, spun in a full circle, and dropped to one knee, bringing the tip of his sword to Coriander's chest. The prince cut off with an 'oof' of expelled air, which became a struggling, choking laugh.

"You are dead, my prince," Leon announced sarcastically. He helped Coriander to his feet.

"Considering I survived," Coriander began, wiping the sweat and dirt from his body with his discarded shirt. Leon mirrored him. "I think open war is a bit extreme." Also considering he knew the truth, if not the exact reason, of what had really happened.

"I tend to agree," Leon replied, his voice muffled through the cloth as he wiped his face, "but there must be some kind of response. Ultimately, it'll be your father's decision."

Coriander sighed deeply. Now, considering this 'attempted assassination' by a foreign kingdom, his father had tightened restrictions on him further. It took every ounce of Coriander's charisma to convince his father that a guard in his room to watch over him while he slept was over the top.

Not that it really bothered him too much—not after Samuel had confided in him what had actually happened. Samuel knew nothing of Shyne, of course, but Coriander had understood his description of 'the intruder' well enough. He had convinced the chamberlain to keep it to himself for now.

He remembered those few hours after his fever broke, in the middle of the night, when Samuel had told him what he had seen and his part in the rescue. The chamberlain had also broken down and cried for nearly an hour as the prince held him. He confided to Coriander what he had suffered from the banished guard. It had been a harrowing tale that truly made Coriander consider whether the gallows would have been the better punishment for the banished man.

Coriander felt very little anger toward Shyne. Mostly, he was full of heartbreak now. How could he have done this to Coriander? Was the sickness a punishment for breaking the contract? If so, what would happen now?

These thoughts weighed heavily on his mind, and Leon must have seen or felt it. He grabbed Coriander's shoulders and looked his friend in the eyes. His new eye looked so perfect it was almost scary.

"Don't worry, Cory," Leon said, his voice steady and firm. "We'll get to the bottom of this, and those responsible will pay. You've got the whole kingdom behind you—don't forget that."

That's what Coriander was afraid of.

Shyne rose from the waters of the little pond. It was one of a dwindling number of true natural places left in this world. He nearly spat in disgust. The humans ruined everything they touched.

Being of such natural wonder, he could use it as a portal to the fey lands. Or, as he had been doing for the last couple of days, he could call upon the well of magic such places held. He looked down at his arm and chest. The burns from the cursed iron bane were gone, healed by the magic of the pond.

What had he been thinking, allowing himself to become entangled with a mortal like that? If Queen Ti...

Something dry snapped nearby. Shyne's eyes narrowed as he scanned the silent forest. The stillness was unnatural, oppressive. A prickle of unease crept up his spine, every instinct screaming that something was amiss. His wings beat, and he leapt into the air and...

...right into the trap.

Netting dropped from the branches above. He tried to shrink and slip through the gaps in the netting, but the moment the iron wires brushed against his skin, a searing pain shot through his entire body. It felt as if his very essence were being torn apart by the cruel touch of the iron bane.

He slammed back into the ground a few moments later, crying out from the pain of the impact and the burns. The netting was made of thin iron wires, each thread biting into his skin like the sting of a thousand needles.

Feet rushed up to him. He tried to struggle, but all his strength was gone. They slapped iron shackles on his wrists and ankles, then stepped back.

The three men were dressed in clothing that had leaves and twigs sewn into them for camouflage. Their faces were either painted or splattered with mud, Shyne couldn't tell.

One of the men stepped closer, his silhouette looming over Shyne as he squatted down with a twisted grin. In that cruel smile, Shyne noticed two things: the jagged gaps where teeth should have been, and the fresh new ones that protruded almost comically from the front.

The iron netting wasn't just a physical trap; it was a symbol of the inescapable chains Shyne had forged for himself. He had tried to play both sides—mortal and fey—but now the consequences of his divided loyalty were tightening around him like the iron wires burning his skin.

"Well," the man said through what seemed like an unfamiliar lisp, "who's the rabbit now, fairy?"

Chapter Twenty-Two

Coriander was trapped somewhere dark—but not completely, he realized. Slivers of light pierced through the undulating cracks in the walls, casting a vivid red glow on the pale pink surface wherever they touched. The darkness pressed in on him, thick and suffocating, broken only by these thin slivers of light that seemed to pulse with every breath he took. Panic threatened to overtake him as he strained to hear beyond the oppressive silence, his ears catching the faintest murmur of voices in the distance.

As his eyes adjusted to the dim light, the muffled voices grew clearer, approaching steadily.

"Yeah, and now what we gonna do with 'im?" a rough man's voice asked.

"Sell 'im!" another man answered quickly.

"An' who's gonna buy that?" the first man spat.

"Shut it!" a third voice interjected. His voice had a strange lisp, as if his teeth were too big for his mouth. "I got plans for this 'un." There was a pause, then a sudden shout, "Eh! What you got in your hands, fairy!"

Fear gripped Coriander's heart as he realized the gravity of his situation. The men's voices grew clearer, and with each word, a new wave of dread washed over him. The idea of being sold—or worse—left him cold. But Shyne's voice, so close and reassuring, reignited a spark of hope within him. He wasn't alone in this.

"Find the prince," Shyne's voice whispered in Coriander's ear. Light bloomed around him as the walls of his cage vanished, and he was suddenly thrown into the air. He soared skyward, and the scene below came into sharp focus.

Shyne was locked in a barred cage at the back of a small wagon, surrounded by three men in rough-spun clothing. A small camp of ramshackle tents stood around a fire pit. The air inside the cage was stale, carrying the acrid scent of sweat and smoke. The walls around him felt almost alive, shifting and groaning as if they were breathing. He saw one of the men yelling and pointing while the other two grabbed crossbows, quickly taking aim at Coriander.

The bolts whizzed past, close enough that the rush of wind sent him tumbling, his wings fluttering frantically as he struggled to regain control. He caught himself and continued to sail away, climbing higher until he rose above the treetops.

For as far as his eyes could see, a forest stretched out beneath him. He soared toward the setting sun, the landscape blurring below. A mix of relief and urgency surged through him as the familiar grotto finally came into view far below. It took him a moment to recognize the area, as he had never seen it from such a height. But he identified the curve of the pond and the little babbling brook that fed the small waterfall.

Then he turned, heading in a now familiar direction. The countryside rolled away slowly beneath him, revealing familiar villages and towns. The sun dipped lower and lower, the warmth of its rays giving way to the cool, silvery light of the moon, which now guided his flight. Still, a strange sense of foreboding gnawed at him. The castle—once a symbol of safety—now felt like a maze of secrets, each corner hiding something he wasn't yet prepared to face. The closer he got, the heavier his wings felt, as if the very air around him was thickening with unseen danger.

Soon the capital came into sight, its streets lit with torches and a few windows still bearing candlelight. He sailed above the rooftops to the castle, rising higher until he squeezed into a small gap between two shutters. The room inside was intimately familiar.

It was HIS room.

Soft firelight lit the room, a barrier against the cold of the night. He circled above the large bed, and he could make out the two forms tangled together in blissful sleep. He circled and dove, coming to rest on the chest of...

Coriander jolted awake, his breath coming in heavy gasps, sweat clinging to his skin. Samuel mumbled quietly beside him, the young man's arm momentarily squeezing the prince's stomach before going limp again.

Something tickled against Coriander's chest. When he brushed it away, his fingers closed around something large and soft. He lifted it between his fingers, peering at it in the dim firelight.

It was a butterfly.

Coriander stared at it in confusion. Its wings, deep crimson and glittering faintly in the dim firelight, flapped weakly a couple more times before going still. Each wing was emblazoned with a large, deep green circle. It was like...

Red hair and green eyes!

A surge of fear gripped Coriander's heart, twisting his gut. Shyne was in trouble! The dream had been real—a message from Shyne! He had been so caught up in his own confusion, so distracted, that he hadn't been paying attention. And now, the consequences were coming to light.

"What is it, Cory?" Samuel asked sleepily beside him, rubbing his eyes.

The prince took a few deep breaths to calm himself, then replied, "Nothing. Just a bad dream." He leaned over and gave Samuel's forehead a gentle kiss. "Go back to sleep."

"Mmm." Samuel groaned softly and drifted off again.

Coriander slipped from the bed, dressing quickly. As he fastened his clothing, he hesitated, glancing back at Samuel. The young man's face was softened in sleep, peaceful and unburdened. For a brief, selfish moment, Coriander felt the urge to crawl back into bed, to lose himself in the comfort of another's warmth. But the urgency gnawing at him was too strong to ignore. He gave Samuel one last fleeting glance, then left the room quietly.

Down the hall, two guards stood with their backs to him, flanking the T-intersection. Coriander took a few steps toward them, then slipped into another door on the hall's opposite wall.

The room was pitch-black, the long-closed shutters barely admitting a sliver of moonlight. In the faint shafts of silver light, he found a striker and quickly lit a candle. The small flame flickered uncertainly, casting long shadows that danced across the room.

Much of the furniture had been covered long ago, and a thick layer of dust lay on nearly everything. Long before Coriander was born, this room had been a study, back when these chambers belonged to his father. But the king had had another wing of the royal quarters remodeled many years ago, and now he resided there.

As a child, Coriander had played in the study a few times, but it had never really been used. Since then, it had been mostly abandoned and forgotten.

He remembered now and cursed himself for forgetting about it. He could have gotten out so many times by now.

His fingers nimbly danced in the space between the wall and the bookcase until they found the hard knot. He pressed against it, and with a low click, the bookcase sprang forward a bare inch. He pulled it open further, and stale, dusty air greeted his nose, carrying with it the scent of long-forgotten secrets.

As Coriander descended the stone stairs, the air grew colder, the dampness clinging to his skin. The only sound was the faint crackle of the torch, its light barely penetrating the thick darkness around him. The walls seemed to close in, the passage narrowing as if to swallow him whole. He pushed forward, determined, but the weight of the silence pressed against him, a stark contrast to the warmth and comfort he had just left behind.

Cobwebs clung thickly to the passageway, a testament to its long-forgotten state. His torch burned through them as he continued forward.

It was an old servant's passage, allowing quick access to what had been the king's study long ago. Probably made for a good escape route in an emergency too. It had once connected to servant's quarters, but those too had been moved during the castle's renovations. The passage now led to a dusty storage room, cluttered with disused furniture and forgotten relics.

A few items clattered to the floor as he opened the concealed door at the bottom of the stairs. This side of the passage was disguised as a false wall, cluttered with cleaning instruments carelessly leaned against it.

Navigating the rest of the corridors and avoiding the few patrolling guards was simple enough. Each step through the passage felt heavier than the last, the weight of his responsibilities pressing down on him. Shyne needed him—of that he was certain. But what about

Leon? Coriander's thoughts drifted to the knight, to the easy camaraderie they once shared. Was he putting that at risk by dragging Leon into this? His duty as a prince warred with his personal loyalties, and for a moment, he wondered if he was making the right choice. But the image of Shyne's green eyes, so full of life, banished any lingering doubts. He had to see this through.

Soon he found himself at the knight's barracks, specifically in front of the door that led to Leon's room.

He silently unlatched the door and slipped inside, closing it softly behind him.

"So you've finally given in to my irresistible wiles, my sultry kitchen wench!" Leon's voice called out from behind him. Coriander turned.

The room was softly lit with several low-burning candles. A decent-sized bed took up one wall, and a dresser and desk dominated the other. Standing in the center of the room was Leon.

Naked, with his back to Coriander, the knight was flexing his arms next to his head to show off his impressive muscles. The sight left the prince speechless, torn between laughter and, he had to admit, a flicker of desire.

"I know I've left you speechless at the sight of me, my desirous dove, but..." Leon turned slowly, his eyes widening in surprise as they found Coriander. "...Cory!" He stood there a few silent seconds, his arms still flexing and his manhood doing the same. "Well," Leon said at last, "you're not quite as pretty as Isabella, but you'll do in a pinch." His grin faded slightly as he noticed the intensity in Coriander's eyes. "Cory... what's going on?" The playfulness in his voice was still there, but tinged with concern. Leon was many things, but he wasn't oblivious, and Coriander's tension was palpable.

Coriander felt the blush heating his cheeks, but he took a deep breath, steeling his nerves and trying to push aside his confusing desire. This was still his best friend, after all. When he finally spoke, his voice was firm, weighted with the gravity of the situation.

"Leon, I need your help."

Chapter Twenty-Three

Having finished his story, Coriander and Leon rode in silence, the rhythmic clop of their horses' hooves the only sound in the still night air. The knight had helped him slip out of the city, and they were now riding to the grotto on borrowed horses since Gemstone and Zedd would have been too easily recognized.

Coriander studied the look on his friend's face but couldn't discern his thoughts. Leon's face was relaxed, his eyes cast slightly downward as if lost in thought, yet his expression revealed nothing. The silence stretched on, growing heavier with each passing moment. Coriander's patience frayed at the edges, his mind racing with possible outcomes, until at last, Leon broke the stillness.

"You know, Cory, if it were anyone else but you, I'd never believe such a tale."

"But you'll still help, right?" Coriander asked cautiously.

Leon's expression faltered for just a second, a flash of hurt crossing his eyes before he nodded firmly. "Even if by some chance this is a fantastic fairy tale you've delusionally crafted, you still need my help one way or the other."

Coriander gave the knight a warm, appreciative smile, choosing to ignore his friend's playful jab that he might just be crazy. Leon's eyes twinkled in response, acknowledging the prince's dodging of his wordplay.

The night was cool, a soft breeze rustling the leaves in the trees that lined the narrow path. The moonlight filtered through the canopy, casting dappled shadows on the ground, adding an air of quiet tension to their journey. It was peaceful, almost too peaceful, as if the world itself was holding its breath, waiting for the storm that was sure to come.

"So," Leon paused, letting the syllable hang in the air a moment, "you and Samuel, huh?" Coriander blushed furiously to Leon's great delight. "Now that," Leon continued, emboldened by his friend's embarrassment, "sounds like a storybook. 'The Prince and the Chamberlain.'" He spread his hands before him as if unrolling a huge banner in the sky.

Coriander tried to kick him off his horse, but Leon just laughed and steered his horse a little further away.

"Sorry... sorry!" the knight squeezed out between ragged breaths of laughter. Coriander just glowered at his friend. Leon took a few deep breaths to steady himself. Then, the laughter faded, and for a moment, the only sound was the steady clop of the horses' hooves on the dirt path. Coriander could feel the weight of Leon's gaze, though the knight's eyes remained fixed ahead.

Finally, Leon spoke, his voice quieter, more tentative than before. "It just makes me a bit jealous."

Coriander's heart skipped a beat at Leon's words. He hadn't allowed himself to fully consider what Leon meant to him—not just as a friend, but as something more. And now, with his mind so consumed by the stranger, everything felt even more confusing. Could he really care for both? Or was he simply clinging to the comfort of familiarity?

As it was, Coriander stopped breathing for a moment. Leon was looking ahead, his face a mask once more.

Coriander wasn't sure what to say, a mix of surprise and uncertainty knotting in his chest. He had always known Leon to be loyal, but this was different—this was personal, intimate. He hadn't even really given this any thought since that night at camp. He had chalked it up to Leon's drunkenness, but now an old phrase danced through his thoughts: 'A drunk man's words are a sober man's thoughts.'

"You don't even have to say anything." Leon's voice was soft but broke the silence like a hammer.

"You've had so much going on, obviously, and there has been no real reason for me to add to it."

"Leon..." Coriander started.

"No, no," Leon interrupted with a shake of his head, "it's selfish of me to pile my own feelings on top of you. I never want to burden you like that."

Coriander's hand shot out, seizing the reins of Leon's horse with a firmness that surprised even him. His heart pounded in his chest as he brought them both to a sudden stop, the intensity of his emotions reflected in the tight grip on the leather reins. He turned to face the knight, his voice deadly serious. "You are never a burden to me." For once, Leon was the one who blushed, caught off guard by the seriousness and compassion in Coriander's voice. "That night at camp, the only reason, THE ONLY REASON, I turned you down is because we were both drunk, and I couldn't be certain either of us was thinking straight."

Leon barked out a laugh, the sound abrupt and sharp. "Well, I can assure you I wasn't." He waggled his eyebrows at Coriander, mischief dancing in his eyes.

The prince sighed and punched the knight in the arm, eliciting another sharp laugh. "Seriously, Leon, once this is all over, we should sit down... really talk."

"It's a date." Leon smiled, then his eyes hardened. "Now let's go rescue your fairy boyfriend."

Coriander sighed, a mixture of relief and apprehension settling in his chest. There was still so much ahead of them, so many uncertainties, but for now, he clung to the hope that together, they could face whatever came next.

By the time they reached the grotto, the sun was beginning to rise, painting the sky with yellow and orange hues. The forest was shrouded in an eerie stillness, as if even the wind had abandoned it. The dense foliage beyond the grotto was too thick for the horses, so they tied them up, ensuring they had access to food and water. Besides, the horses would have been too loud; they needed silence when approaching the bandit camp.

They packed what they needed, including the heavy crossbow Leon had brought, and began their trek east. The forest seemed to close in around them, the shadows deepening with every step. The usual sounds of birds and insects had vanished, leaving only the crunch of leaves beneath their boots and the occasional snap of a twig. Coriander's breath came shallow and quick, his heart pounding in rhythm with the silence that threatened to engulf them.

It was difficult to gauge exact distances from the butterfly's vision, but Coriander felt he hadn't traveled far in the dream before reaching the grotto. Doubt gnawed at him as they crept closer to the clearing. Was this the right choice? Could they really take on these bandits and survive? But with every step, he pushed those thoughts aside, knowing that hesitation could mean the difference between life and death—not just for him, but for Leon and Shyne as well.

Leon took the lead, his crossbow loaded and ready. He'd likely only get one shot with it, as reloading wasn't something he could do quickly. Even with his strength, resetting the string required the stirrup and all his might. The weapon was powerful, but it was far from convenient.

They each carried their swords as well. Coriander was relatively sure there were only three bandits at the camp. If they could get one with the crossbow, the other two should be easy to dispatch with their swords.

Relatively? If? Easily? Each word felt like a harbinger, as if something was bound to go terribly wrong. Coriander shook away the negative thoughts. This wasn't the time. The plan would work.

As expected, it only took a couple of hours to reach the clearing where the bandits were holed up. From their position, Coriander spotted the wagon and the cage holding Shyne, now draped in a thick patchwork of blankets that seemed to muffle even the sounds within. The bandits' tent stood nearby, but there was no sign of the ne'er-do-wells.

Leon tapped Coriander on the shoulder, signaling for him to move around the edge of the clearing toward the cage. The prince nodded and began to creep forward, his heart hammering in his chest.

"...of course. Right this way," a gruff voice spoke suddenly. Coriander froze, having only made it a few feet away from Leon.

From the far side of the tent, three bandits appeared, two of them flanking their leader and a large portly man in poorly kept fine clothes. Two other men in light armor followed them. Coriander cursed under his breath, his heart sinking as the situation grew more complicated than he'd anticipated.

The bandit leader led the portly man over to the cage. He pulled the cloth covering it off and stood in a '*ta-da*' gesture.

The portly man studied the nude figure in the cage for a few moments, his voice greasy and low as he spoke. "And how do I know he is the genuine article?" The leader responded by picking up a long metal rod leaned against the wagon.

Shyne slid back in the cage, getting as far away from the bandit as he possibly could without touching the bars. The bandit jammed the long rod between the bars, touching it against the fairy's thighs.

Shyne's scream was a gut-wrenching, animalistic sound that cut through the stillness like a knife. A puff of smoke rose from the brief contact, and Coriander nearly broke from cover right then. But it would do no good to rush in now. It would only get them killed.

"Good!" the large man wheezed. "Very good!"

"Then you'll honor our agreement?" The bandit leader rasped between his too-big front teeth.

"Certainly! Such a small thing to grant for such a great prize!" He turned to his men. "Go retrieve the horses and hook them to this wagon. We leave immediately!"

The two armored men bowed and walked off, disappearing behind the tent again. From his vantage point, Coriander could just make them out walking down an overgrown path about the width of the wagon.

He turned to Leon, making an impatient gesture as he loosened his sword in its scabbard. It was definitely now or never. Leon nodded agreement and readied the crossbow.

"See, boys?" the bandit leader exalted to his men, "Full pardons as promised. Now we can…"

He stopped suddenly with a gurgle, his hands reaching up to find a long, thin shaft of wood sticking out of his neck, its end tipped with small colorful feathers.

Coriander hadn't even heard the crossbow go off, but at the sight of the bolt in the leader's neck, he drew his sword and leapt forward into the clearing with a cry. Leon followed behind him.

The portly man screamed and tried to duck beneath the wagon, but its low build wouldn't allow all his bulk to squeeze underneath. One of the bandits drew his sword and turned to meet their charge. The other dove for cover into the tent. The leader ran his fingertips along the fletching of the bolt in disbelief.

Coriander and Leon charged the armed bandit. Despite his desperate defense, he was slowly losing ground against the combined force of the knight and prince.

There was the sudden sharp sound of a firing crossbow, and Leon yelled in pain, a small bolt sticking out of his thigh. The other bandit stepped free of the tent and drew his sword as he tossed the crossbow aside.

Leon staggered but, with grim determination, turned to face the new threat. As the pressure fell off the first bandit, his defense tightened, and he was no longer losing ground against the prince.

Coriander pushed harder, raining furious, hammering blows against the bandit. Finally, the man made a critical mistake, and he screamed as Coriander severed his arm just below the elbow. The bandit dropped to his knees, cradling the squirting stump. The prince's next swing put the man out of his misery as the blade split his skull.

As he spun to check on Leon, sudden blinding pain exploded in his own mind. The world spun, and he was suddenly tasting blood and dirt. Coriander's eyes rolled, and his vision went dangerously dark before finally settling on extremely fuzzy. He couldn't get his body to move through the disorientation and pain.

Through his blurred vision, he could make out Leon, still engaged with the crossbow bandit. But now, stalking toward the pair was the leader, the bolt still protruding from his neck, and the long iron rod gleaming in his hands.

Coriander struggled to shout a warning, but all that escaped his lips was a low, guttural moan. Desperation clawed at him as he tried to move, but his body refused to obey. The leader's shadow fell over him, and in that moment, Coriander knew that he was powerless to stop the onslaught. All he could do was watch as the iron rod was raised high, the final blow ready to descend, with Leon still locked in a desperate battle only a few feet away. Darkness edged his vision, and Coriander's last thought was a silent plea for a miracle that he knew might never come.

Chapter Twenty-Four

The bandit who had once held the crossbow dashed forward, swinging his sword in a wild arc. He was sloppy, untrained, and telegraphed the move pathetically. Leon simply sidestepped the swing, his sword flashing in response. Blood arced into the air as the crossbow bandit fell to his knees, screaming and trying to hold his spilling entrails in.

Even in his dazed state, still struggling to remain conscious, Coriander felt pride swell in his heart. Leon was, after all, a knight of the realm. Young, certainly, but massively talented. He had taken to knighthood like a fish to water, yet beneath that pride, a creeping fear gnawed at Coriander—what if Leon wasn't fast enough, strong enough? Coriander's heart pounded, not just from the injury but from the helplessness gnawing at him. He was supposed to be a prince, someone people could rely on, and yet here he was—useless, watching as Leon fought for both their lives.

The bandit leader seized his moment, raising the iron rod high above his head as he closed in, his eyes locked on Leon with murderous intent. Leon spun, almost impossibly fast, his sword meeting the iron rod with a resounding clash, effectively blocking the blow.

Leon's other hand shot up, grabbing the head of the bolt sticking out of the leader's neck, and ripped it free. The leader screamed, but it was mostly a muffled gurgle. His eyes narrowed in anger as he bore down harder with the iron bar.

So Leon, Knight of the Kingdom, buried the crossbow bolt into the man's eye. The scream burst clearly through the blood in his throat as the leader stumbled back, dropping the rod. His hands grasped the bolt and ripped it free, the eye still impaled on it. The bandit dropped to his knees, pale and breathing wetly. Blood sprayed from his lips as he looked up at Leon, his mouth shaping an unmistakable curse, the sound a wet, garbled whisper.

The tip of the knight's sword slid easily into the bandit's chest, puncturing his heart. He burbled one last curse before collapsing dead.

Leon looked like he was about to make a snide remark, but his eyes suddenly widened, and he ducked. A horse burst into the camp from behind the tent, its rider swinging a large axe at the knight. It missed scalping Leon by bare inches. Coriander's heart skipped a beat as he saw a few strands of Leon's dark hair scatter in the wind, the near miss sending a jolt of fear through him.

Turning his duck into a sweep, Leon scooped up the iron rod and let the maneuver take him to the ground. As his ass planted on the ground, he threw the rod like a spear. It slammed into the armored chest of the second rider just as he cleared the tent and took him from the horse.

Numbness receded from Coriander's hands and feet, allowing him to wiggle his fingers and toes, but the rest of his body remained frustratingly unresponsive. He could speak, but only in a hoarse whisper. But he didn't need to shout a warning as the first rider spun his horse to bear down again on Leon.

Leon turned to meet the threat. A foot soldier without a bow or spear was at a huge disadvantage against a mounted opponent. The mercenary knew this too, and pressed his advantage, charging the knight with the axe held high for the assured killing blow.

However, Leon had no intention of holding his ground against the attack. As soon as the horse was close enough to be committed, the knight dove to the side, away from the horseman's axe. The horse passed through the space he'd just been, crashing into the other mercenary just as he was getting to his feet.

There was the sickening sound of breaking bones and screams as the two mercenaries and the horse went down in a tangled pile. The night was thick with the smell of blood and sweat, the air cool against Coriander's feverish skin. Shadows flickered and danced in the firelight, casting the camp in an eerie glow. Every sound felt amplified—the distant rustling of leaves, the crackling of the fire, the wet gasps of the dying men.

The horse got to its feet the quickest, stepping on and breaking one of the mercenary's legs. A wild kick as the horse sprang away hit the other mercenary in the chest.

At that point, Leon put both men down with very little fight from them. With a quick swipe to clean his sword, Leon sheathed it in one fluid motion.

He walked over and knelt down to take a look at Coriander. "That's going to be quite a goose egg," he remarked, reaching out. Whatever spot he touched on Coriander's head flared in pain, and the prince's stomach churned. Leon's usual bravado slipped for just a moment as he looked down at Coriander. His eyes softened, the hardness from the fight melting away. "You gave me a scare, you know that?" he muttered, his voice low but not without a hint of relief.

Leon helped him sit up, and the world spun, his vision darkening again. It shrank to the tiniest pinpoint of light before slowly returning.

"Slow and deep breaths," Leon told him, leaning him back against an empty crate. Coriander complied, his vision starting to clear and his stomach beginning to settle.

"St...st...stop!" a nearby voice cracked, high and squeaky. Leon turned to regard the portly man, who had come out from his hiding spot beneath the wagon. He was brandishing the sword of the bandit Coriander had killed, the severed hand still clung to the handle. Leon started to rise, his hand reaching for his own sword.

"D...don't move!" the man stammered, taking a step back and bumping into the wagon. "I'll...I'll..."

He never finished the sentence. A hand grabbed his greasy hair and slammed his head against the bars. Shyne's other hand shot out, pressing something small against the man's neck. He dragged it across the flesh, ripping and tearing the skin unevenly. Blood sprayed in rapid spurts, and the man fell to the ground, writhing and dying.

Shyne dropped the rusty nail, the skin of his palm and fingers smoking and blackened. The rest of him looked just as terrible, with similar burns across his gaunt and bony frame. His face was sunken, making his eyes look huge and inhuman. His short red hair was missing in patches that were covered in dark burns.

Whatever curse or magic was at work, it was beyond anything they had faced before.

Leon retrieved the horseman's axe and strolled over to the cage. Shyne recoiled as far from the edge closest to the knight as he could. This seemed to bring Leon some sort of satisfaction as he pointed the axe at the fairy.

"Understand this," he breathed in a dangerous voice, "you're only getting free because this man," he pointed at Coriander, "cares about you for some ungodly reason."

Shyne nodded in understanding. Satisfied, Leon raised the axe and brought it down hard on the padlock holding the door. The lock shattered, pieces flying everywhere.

"That's a good axe!" Leon gave the weapon an appreciative look over before throwing open the door to the cage. He returned to Coriander's side. "How's it looking, buddy?"

Coriander tried to shake his head and nearly toppled over. "No good," he blurted.

Behind them, Shyne crawled from the wagon. Placing his feet on the ground, he pushed himself out and immediately collapsed. Leon gave him an annoyed look.

"You too, huh?" Leon's tone was light, but there was a hard edge to it. He had seen men fall to lesser wounds, and yet Shyne still stood—if only barely. Whatever drove the fairy, it was strong, maybe stronger than Leon could understand.

Shyne returned the annoyed look. "You have to get us to the grotto," he croaked.

"And why…"

"Do it, Leon," Coriander interrupted, his eyes pleading.

Leon sighed and stood, his eyes scanning the camp. They needed to move quickly, but with both Coriander and Shyne injured, time was not on their side. The shadows around them felt heavier, as if danger still lurked just beyond sight. A riderless horse neighed nearby, and Leon knew what to do.

Chapter Twenty-Five

Leon led the horses carefully through the thick underbrush. It was a slow and treacherous journey. Both the prince and the fairy had passed out almost immediately once he'd gotten them into the saddles. He had used a bit of rope he found in the camp to lash them both into place so they wouldn't fall during the trip.

He had also tightly tied a bit of ripped cloth around his thigh. The bleeding had stopped, but it hurt like hell to walk on.

It had taken him nearly three times as long to finally reach the hidden pond of the grotto on the way back. The evening was growing darker and much colder. He wouldn't be surprised if the first snows of the season began in the next few weeks.

The grotto was a hidden sanctuary, it's still waters reflecting the deepening twilight. The air was thick with the scent of damp earth and ancient magic, a place where the mundane world seemed to fade away, leaving only whispers of forgotten power. The fairy seemed to revive almost as soon as they reached the grotto. He struggled against the ropes holding him in place for a moment, and then growled, "Release me."

Leon almost laughed. The air of command in the fairy's voice was humorous to him. He slid an iron dagger from his belt, considering for a moment that maybe he should bury it in the fairy's heart and be done with it.

Shyne's eyes widened at the sight of the dagger and the dark look on the knight's face. "I can heal him! He might die otherwise!" he begged.

Leon's grip tightened on the dagger's hilt as Cory's stories with Shyne flooded his mind—the deceit, the manipulation, the pain. Yet, there was Coriander's life hanging in the balance. Leon wasn't a man who easily forgave, but this was different. This was about loyalty, not just to Coriander, but to the kingdom. With a frustrated growl, he cut the ropes, the dagger flashing as it parted the bindings.

"Why do you think you're still alive?" Leon growled, moving to cut the ropes binding Coriander. The prince was still breathing steadily but had yet to awaken during the trip. Part of his skull was swollen, so much so that it gave him an uneven profile.

He gathered Coriander in his arms, carrying him to the pond. He pushed his way through the reeds, scattering dragonflies and other insects. Splashing into the water nearly to his knees, Leon sat the unconscious body of his friend into the shallows.

Shyne slowly dismounted from the horse, which greeted him with a concerned whinny. He scratched it soothingly. His emaciated body could barely hold itself up, and each step toward the pond felt like a journey of ages. Finally, he reached the edge as Leon was stepping out.

"I can heal your leg too," Shyne whispered as he passed. Leon's face hardened immediately.

"While I appreciate the last healing you provided me, and the return of my eye, I know the price of dealing with a fairy now. I'd rather cut my eye out with a dull spoon than incur a debt to you."

Shyne truly looked guilty at Leon's words. In his weakened state, he had hoped for a moment of redemption, a chance to prove he wasn't the enemy Leon believed him to be. But the knight's rejection only reinforced his isolation. He swallowed the bitterness, forcing himself to focus on the task at hand—the one thing he could do to make amends. "It wouldn't..."

"No," Leon interrupted with finality. He began to unpack the horses they had brought here and set up a camp.

Shyne shrugged weakly, and then lowered himself into the water next to the unconscious Coriander. The cool water seemed to seep into his bones now that there was so little flesh to hold it back. The cold mud at the bottom caressed and conformed to his body. He could already feel the trickle of life flowing back into him.

"Must you sit so close to him?" Leon demanded, glaring down at him.

"No," Shyne croaked his reply. "I must actually sit closer." With the knight glaring down at him, he slid his body against the prince's, pulling him into an embrace and laying Coriander's head against his chest.

Leon looked ready to argue, but before he could speak, Shyne whispered an ancient word of power in the Sylvan tongue. The air in the grotto seemed to vibrate with unseen energy. A warm, golden light began to emanate from the pond, the water rippling as if stirred by an invisible hand. Tiny motes of energy lifted off its surface, floating for a moment in the air, and then popping like bubbles.

As the golden light spread through the water, Shyne felt a twinge of fear. The process was delicate, and any disruption could spell disaster. His concentration wavered for a moment, his mind racing with thoughts of what might go wrong—what if Leon's suspicion led him to act? What if Coriander was too far gone? The pond's light flickered, but Shyne steadied himself, refusing to let doubt take hold. Now the life energy rushed into Shyne like a torrent, filling the emptiness inside left by the iron bane. However, he had to fight to steady the flow, as too much too fast could cause just as much damage. Once he was absorbing it at a safe speed, he began sharing it with the prince.

Even in his unconscious state, Coriander let out a deep, grateful sigh as the healing energies began to flow into him. Shyne could actually feel it beginning to mend the prince's injuries. He also felt just how close the prince was to death. Another hour or so, and this wouldn't have worked at all. The swelling in his head would have been too much to fix. He kept that information to himself.

"How long will this take?" Leon's demanding voice was a little softer, more awestruck.

Shyne cracked open one eye to glare at the knight. "A day, give or take a few hours. Longer, if I keep being interrupted."

Leon's eyes hardened again at the fairy's flippancy. "I only ask so I can prepare for what's ahead. The prince's absence is going to be noticed, again, and this time I'm not there to convince the knight captain to let me retrieve him myself. There is a good chance we could have a score of knights searching for us come the 'morrow."

Shyne's expression softened slightly. He nodded, "I will do my best to hurry."

As Shyne focused on the healing, Leon couldn't shake the feeling that something was watching them, waiting. The forest was too quiet, the air too still. With Coriander's life hanging in the balance, they couldn't afford any more surprises. And yet, deep down, Leon knew their troubles were far from over.

"You said a day, fairy."

"And it has only been sixteen hours, human," Shyne snapped, frustration evident in his voice. The knight's impatience grated on him, but he remained focused on his task. Coriander was no worse, but he was no better either.

Shyne had yet to reveal the full truth to Leon: the prince had been teetering on the brink of death. His body was fighting the healing, a cruel balance of life and decay. It was a battle that drained every ounce of Shyne's magic, barely keeping Coriander from slipping away.

Leon's boots sank into the soft earth as he paced along the shoreline, carving a deepening trench in the damp ground. His eyes darted anxiously toward the horizon. "The knights could arrive any moment. When they do, we're in real trouble!"

"You don't fully grasp the danger," Shyne muttered, his gaze darkening with an edge of warning.

Leon stopped abruptly, frustration etched into his features. "What do you mean?"

Shyne took a deep breath, his expression shifting to one of grave seriousness. "The prince's condition is critical. His body is resisting the healing, and if we don't act swiftly, he may not survive."

"But it was just a bump on the head!" Leon's voice cracked with disbelief. "It can't be that severe!" When Shyne's silence stretched, he grasped at any possible solution. "Can't you use one of those magical mushrooms on him?"

"I could, if I had access to the Feylands to fetch one. But the journey would take too long. He'd be gone before I could return."

"Could I go?"

"No." Shyne's laugh was hollow. "There are too many reasons why that's impossible," he said, cutting off Leon's inevitable 'Why?' before it could escape.

"Well, if the knights arrive," Leon's voice dropped to a dangerous edge, "they'll either kill you on sight or rip Cory from your arms and drag him home."

"And that will kill him."

Leon's frustration boiled over as he threw up his hands. "What can we do?"

Shyne's eyes softened with reluctant consideration. "There might be a solution…" he murmured, almost to himself.

"What?" Leon demanded, desperation in his tone.

Shyne shook his head, his expression pained. "You won't like it."

Leon fell to his knees, the muddy ground squelching beneath him. Tears welled in his eyes, his frustration morphing into raw, unfiltered emotion. He pointed a trembling finger at Shyne. "Don't tell me what I might or might not like, you fairy-tale bastard." His finger shifted to Coriander. "I will do anything for him!"

Love, pure and undeniable. Shyne's heart ached, touched by the knight's devotion. It was a rare and precious thing, even if it was born from friendship or something deeper. Perhaps, if Leon's conviction was strong enough, it could be the key to saving the prince.

"I can't speed up the healing," Shyne explained, his voice firm but gentle. "But I might be able to create a doppelganger to take the prince's place until he recovers."

Leon's face darkened with uncertainty. The idea clearly unsettled him. Shyne watched as conflicted emotions flashed across his face. After a tense pause, Leon seemed to resolve himself.

"What needs to be done?"

"It must be done through a deal," Shyne said. "It's the only way I can draw enough magic without risking the prince's life."

Leon's eyes narrowed, a mix of skepticism and resolve in his gaze. "What's the cost?"

"You will have to relinquish something that was given to you," Shyne said solemnly, the weight of his words hanging heavy in the air.

Leon's mind raced. Back at the castle, he would have had plenty of options, but here, with only the bare necessities, he had little choice. Except...

He turned to Shyne, whose eyes glistened with an almost alien sadness. The fairy's sorrow seemed almost too human. Shyne motioned for Leon to come closer.

Leon waded through the pond, the cold water sloshing around him as he approached Shyne and Coriander. The prince lay cradled in the fairy's arms, his swollen head a stark contrast to the serene expression on Shyne's face.

"I'm sorry..." Shyne began, his voice trembling with emotion.

"Just do it!" Leon's command was sharp, laced with desperation.

Shyne nodded, reaching up to cup Leon's face with his free hand. The touch was cool and clammy from the pond water, yet it radiated a strange warmth, spreading through Leon's body like a gentle flame. Surprisingly, there was no pain. Instead, darkness began to seep into Leon's right eye, signaling the end of the spell.

With a sweeping motion, Shyne's free hand glowed with a brilliant light. He plucked a single hair from Coriander's head, instantly consumed by the magic. As Shyne chanted in the haunting, melodic language of the Fey, a storm of butterflies erupted around them. Their wings flickered with every color imaginable, forming a swirling vortex of light and motion that gradually descended, revealing a bewildered, naked Coriander.

"Well, this is unusual!" the doppelganger declared, its gaze flitting between the original Coriander and the surrounding scene. "Very unusual," it muttered, its voice tinged with confusion.

"Hear me, changeling," Shyne commanded, his voice carrying an authoritative edge. The doppelganger's eyes locked onto his. "Understand what you are."

The doppelganger took a deep breath, its expression shifting to one of resignation. "I understand and accept my role."

"You will assume the prince's place until he is able to return," Shyne instructed.

"Yes, my master," the doppelganger responded, bowing deeply.

"This will work?" Leon asked, his voice laced with doubt.

"I have all your friend's memories," the doppelganger answered, its voice sending a shiver down Leon's spine. He couldn't shake the uneasy feeling that he might regret this decision.

Leon climbed out of the pond, his movements stiff and deliberate. He rifled through their packs, retrieving the old eye patch he kept as a reminder of past sacrifices. As he slipped it over his darkened eye, the weight of his decision settled heavily on his shoulders.

He and the doppelganger mounted their horses and departed, their silhouettes disappearing into the distance.

Shyne watched them go, his gaze lingering until they were out of sight. With a weary sigh, he turned his full attention back to Coriander and focused on the healing, his heart heavy with the burden of what had transpired.

Chapter Twenty-Six

It took immense effort to open his eyes, as though they were weighed down by a thousand stones. Slowly, his eyelids parted, and he was met with a blinding light that seared his vision, as if the sun itself had been concentrated into a single, painful glare. His head throbbed with an intensity he had never before experienced, and his body moved sluggishly, every action heavy and uncertain.

"Easy, my prince," a soft, and somewhat familiar voice reassured him.

He found himself chest-deep in cool, crystalline water that sparkled with an ethereal light, a sight that seemed to both soothe and bewilder him. As the soothing coolness enveloped him, a wave of confusion and relief mingled with the remnants of his dream. Dragonflies danced languidly around the reeds at the water's edge, their iridescent wings catching the sunlight and casting fleeting rainbows on the surface of the water. The faint buzz of their wings was a delicate counterpoint to the soothing murmur of the stream.

He became acutely aware of the warmth radiating from the body pressed against him, the gentle firmness of Shyne's arms enveloping him in a protective embrace. The sensation of Shyne's closeness offered both comfort and a sense of safety in the midst of his disorientation.

"Shyne?" he rasped, his voice cracking and barely audible, a rough sound that seemed foreign and strained to his own ears.

"Shhh, don't try to speak," Shyne murmured soothingly. Something cool and refreshing touched Coriander's lips, and he instinctively tried to turn away. The unsettling memory of the Nectar lingered in his mind, its cloying sweetness a stark reminder of past events he was desperate to forget. "It's just water," Shyne added gently.

Coriander's tension eased as the cool liquid trickled over his parched lips, each sip quenching the intense dryness that had parched his throat and tongue. The sensation was like a gentle caress, bringing a small but welcome relief to his ravaged senses.

But the sensation of revitalization was fleeting, and soon the soothing warmth of the blanket wrapped around him, and the gentle, rhythmic sound of Shyne's shushing combined to create a cocoon of comfort. Coriander's senses were lulled by the soft embrace of sleep, drawing him back into a tranquil, dreamless rest.

The king's decree echoed with the finality of a hammer striking iron.

Not-Coriander bowed, his defiance extinguished. The decree had fallen like a coffin nail, sealing the fate of all arguments. He understood the desires of his counterpart and had fought for an alternative outcome. Yet the Prince's father remained immovable. The doppelganger prince had no choice but to submit.

As he walked back to Leon, the weight of the decision bore heavily on him. Leon, with his roguish charm marred by the dark eye patch, looked deeply troubled. Leon's hand on his shoulder was a fleeting comfort before he withdrew, the realization of the doppelganger's true identity shadowing his expression.

"I did my best," Not-Coriander said quietly as they exited the throne room.

"I know," Leon replied, his voice tinged with frustration and resignation. "And I don't think Cory would fault you for your efforts."

"Lady Miranda may be the most advantageous choice," the doppelganger conceded, "but it's clear that Coriander's heart lies elsewhere."

Leon shook his head, his gaze hardening. "It's regrettable, but this will proceed regardless of Cory's wishes. The future of the kingdom is at stake."

They navigated the richly adorned halls of the royal quarters, where the ambient light from torches flickered against the stone walls. Guards stood at rigid attention, their presence a stark reminder of the prince's confinement. Their conversation fell into a somber silence as they approached the prince's chamber.

"What worries me is the Iron Crown ceremony." The doppelganger, with the prince's memories, understood the gravity of the event. The ceremony involved the prince and his betrothed wearing matching iron crowns three days before the wedding, transitioning to silver and then gold, symbolizing their ascent into their new roles.

"Lady Miranda won't be here for another two weeks at best. I hope your master can complete Cory's healing by then."

The doppelganger nodded, his mind a whirl of conflicted emotions. The magic that formed him revealed that Shyne had already completed the healing, but he was bound to secrecy. He had so far avoided touching iron, the bane of fairies. It had been a struggle, requiring him to use his royal authority to avoid iron latches. A single touch could unravel the magic sustaining him.

He also knew, thanks to reassurances from his master, that the prince would return in time for the ceremony. Yet, he was forbidden from sharing this crucial information.

For now, he had to maintain the facade. His master had devised a plan, and he was bound to follow it, no matter how conflicted he felt.

Coriander counted off the last few reps, then collapsed onto the blanket, breathing heavily. His bare skin glistened with sweat under the warm sunlight, which was quickly swept away by the cool breeze that rustled the leaves overhead.

Shyne lounged nearby on the rocks by the gurgling waterfall, his emaciated frame a stark contrast to the lush greenery surrounding them. He chewed thoughtfully on an apple, his eyes fixed on Coriander with a mix of detached amusement and lingering concern.

The prince recognized Shyne's deliberate provocation; after all, the fairy didn't need sustenance. When he first emerged from the pond, dazed and disoriented, he'd been irritated by this arrangement. But now, he saw it as a necessary part of their peculiar alliance.

It had been several days—perhaps a week—since Coriander had awoken. His head had healed, but the fog of confusion lingered like a heavy mist. During this time, Shyne had cared for him, though the true origin of the food remained a mystery that gnawed at Coriander's mind.

His clothes, now mere tatters, bore the marks of his ordeal: bloodstains, rips, and the lingering dampness from the pond. He suspected some damage had been inflicted more recently, though he had no way to prove it. Despite this, he cast a sharp, resentful glance at Shyne.

In the days of mental recovery, his body had grown weaker. Their current focus was on restoring his strength.

"Excellent form, my prince," Shyne remarked, his tone casual as he took another bite of the apple.

Coriander's irritation flared. "I told you to stop calling me that. I'm not your property," he snapped, his voice rising with anger. "Don't brush it aside. You exploited my desperation with your deal. You used my friend's safety as leverage and drugged me with your Nectar to cloud my mind."

Shyne's gaze dropped, his voice barely above a murmur. "I didn't realize the Nectar would have such an effect on a human…"

Coriander's hand cut through the air, silencing him. "Regardless, you continued to use it. I felt the contract break when we rescued you. We're even now, so I am no longer 'your prince.'"

While Coriander's words rang true, Shyne had yet to disclose that he had released Coriander from the obligation. The act of saving him alone had not balanced the scales. Shyne chewed thoughtfully on the apple as Coriander continued his tirade.

"So how can I trust you if you keep treating me like your possession?"

Shyne gracefully descended from the rocks, landing lightly in the mud. He took a few deliberate steps and tossed the mostly whole apple to Coriander. The prince caught it with practiced ease. In that fleeting moment, Shyne's wings unfurled with a burst of iridescence. The fairy leaped into the air, spun, and vanished beneath the water with barely a ripple.

Coriander bit into the crisp, tangy apple, the flavor a sharp contrast to the turmoil simmering within him. They had gone through this argument several times, and each time, Shyne had retreated, only to return with another gift for Coriander to reject.

    He reclined on the blanket, savoring the warmth of the sun on his skin and the rare, fleeting peace. The intensity of his anger had faded, replaced by a lingering unease about Shyne. His thoughts meandered as he lay there, contemplating the tangled web of their relationship and the uncertain path that lay ahead.

Chapter Twenty-Seven

He stood there, his feet barely touching the pond's surface. Water dripped freely from his naked body, pattering gently onto the pond below. Gossamer wings, reminiscent of darting dragonflies, fluttered slightly in the breeze. His pale skin glowed in the evening light, each freckle standing out like small constellations. In his hands, gently held, was a bright red clematis flower—a striking match for his blazing hair.

As he emerged from the pond, his wings beat the air, sending droplets of water flying in all directions. His feet seemed to glide across the water's surface, barely leaving a ripple. He came to a stop at the shore, dropping to both knees in a deep bow, extending both hands to offer the flower to the prince.

"I did not know the effect the Nectar would have on you," Shyne's voice was barely a whisper, thick with sorrow and regret. "I should never have used the leverage I had over you to force something you did not want. It was wrong. An abuse of power over what should have been a simple exchange."

He took a deep breath before continuing. "This mistake stems from the lack of wisdom that comes with youth. Thus, I offer you this flower to balance the scales.

This clematis is my flower, from which I was born. It is me, and I am it. For as long as you hold it, I am under your power."

Coriander sat on his blanket next to the fire, contemplating the fairy. Aside from the shallow rise and fall of his chest, Shyne remained perfectly still, his posture a silent testament to his vulnerability.

Coriander's heart ached with the complexity of his emotions. Anger and betrayal mingled with the remnants of his initial desire, leaving him unsure of how to respond. His mind made up, he reached over and gently took the flower from Shyne's open hands. He studied its vibrant color and intricate design before deliberately placing it atop the nearby bedroll.

"Shyne, please sit up." It was a request, not a command. Maybe this counted as an apology, but Coriander wasn't going to indulge in any more fairy games.

Shyne sat up slowly, confusion and hope etched on his face as his eyes darted to the flower lying beside the prince.

"Understand one thing," Coriander said, holding up a finger for emphasis. "I was never unwilling. Yes, you had favor over me for healing Leon. Yes, the Nectar wasn't letting me think straight during our..." Coriander cleared his throat, "...sessions."

"But," he continued, "I had been willing." Coriander sighed, reflecting on the hours Shyne had been absent. The anger he had felt wasn't entirely warranted. He had been just as complacent in the arrangement. "You, however, took advantage of that willingness. You twisted it and made it something foul."

Tears gleamed at the corners of Shyne's eyes. Coriander could see the full remorse there, and it broke something in his heart. He stood and indicated for Shyne to do the same. The fairy obeyed. The prince stepped closer, his hands gently resting on Shyne's shoulders, grounding him in the moment.

"No more games," Coriander said, looking into Shyne's eyes. "No more fey tricks. Tonight, we balance the scales." Shyne's eyes darted to the discarded flower, and Coriander softly guided his face back to meet his gaze with one hand. "No," the prince shook his head, "not like that. Like this."

Coriander leaned forward, pressing his lips to Shyne's in a slow, deliberate kiss. Shyne stiffened at the unexpected contact, then relaxed and began to kiss back.

The kiss, once hesitant, grew fervent, as if it was a silent pact to erase past transgressions. They were soon embraced tightly, their hands roving over each other's soft, bare skin. Shyne gasped sharply as Coriander's lips traced a fiery path along his neck, leaving passionate, lingering kisses. Desire flared anew as their lips and fingers explored each other's skin with increasing fervor.

With a heavy breath, Coriander pressed down on Shyne's shoulders, and Shyne dropped to his knees without hesitation. The prince's throbbing cock hovered inches from Shyne's lips, its tip glistening with pre-cum.

"Please," the prince pleaded breathlessly, his fingers tangling in Shyne's hair. Shyne didn't waste the invitation; his tongue darted out, gliding along the length of Coriander's member. The act elicited a moan from the prince, urging Shyne to continue.

Shyne grasped one of the prince's ass cheeks firmly while gently rubbing his balls with the other hand. He guided the cock between his lips, relishing the sweet taste of pre-cum. With deliberate slowness, he teased the tip with his tongue, drawing out every sensation.

Coriander's breathing grew heavy, small groans escaping his lips as his knees shook from the overwhelming pleasure. He tugged gently on Shyne's hair, signaling his intense enjoyment.

Shyne took more of the cock into his mouth until he felt the tip press against the back of his throat. He held it there for a few seconds, letting the moisture coat the shaft while his tongue worked the tip. Coriander's hips bucked from pleasure, but Shyne held him tight, continuing his ministrations.

As Coriander's breathing and moaning crescendoed, Shyne began to slowly withdraw, his lips creating a gentle suction. In and out, he worked the full length, the wet, sloppy sounds only heightening his own excitement. He increased his speed and pressure, eager to taste the prince's release.

Moments later, with a guttural grunt, Coriander came. The warm fluid surged into the back of Shyne's throat, a burning sensation mingling with its surprising sweetness. Shyne struggled to swallow, his throat working to accommodate the rich taste.

Still savoring the last of Coriander's release, Shyne was taken by surprise when the prince pushed him down onto the blanket. Coriander collapsed on top of him, their lips meeting in a fiery kiss.

Coriander's kisses meandered from Shyne's lips, down his neck, and across his chest, each touch igniting a fiery path of desire. They paused briefly as Coriander kissed, caressed, and sucked on Shyne's erect nipples.

Shyne moaned at the touch, his body flushed with arousal.

Coriander's kisses traveled downward, each touch intensified by his soft, playful chuckles. His lips moved with purpose, igniting a feverish heat in Shyne. They followed the trail of hair down to Shyne's erect cock. A soft kiss on the underside of the head was the only warning before the full length slid into Coriander's warm mouth.

Shyne's cock quickly hit the back of Coriander's throat, the prince's lips applying steady pressure at the base. Shyne's eyes rolled back from the intense sensation, an involuntary moan escaping his lungs.

The sensation lasted only a few seconds before Coriander coughed, but those moments felt like hours to Shyne. His body trembled, and his breathing was ragged. In all his life, he had never felt such pleasure.

After a brief moment to catch his breath, Coriander resumed his efforts. His lips moved with a steady rhythm, applying firm pressure as his tongue danced teasingly around the sensitive tip.

Overwhelmed by the sensations, Shyne cried out in exhilaration as he reached his climax. Coriander took it all, but rather than swallowing, he lifted Shyne's legs, exposing his tight opening. He let the warm, wet life-seed coat Shyne's entrance.

Shyne gasped at the sudden warmth, his mind whirling with the intensity of the moment. Coriander met his gaze, an unspoken promise of shared desire and pleasure. Slowly, Coriander pressed into him, and Shyne welcomed him with matching enthusiasm.

They moved together in a rhythm of slow thrusts, moans, and kisses, their passion extending beyond the sunset and deep into the night.

Chapter Twenty-Eight

They sat together in the cool water of the pond, their bodies lightly brushing against each other. The gentle cascade of the nearby waterfall created a soothing backdrop, its rhythmic gurgle blending with the distant croak of a toad. Dragonflies flitted above their heads, their delicate wings catching the sun's rays. The last few days had been a blissful interlude in each other's company, a respite from the worries of the outside world.

Coriander sipped from his wine, its sweet warmth a comforting contrast to the cool water. Between fits of giggles, he looked at Shyne, who was animatedly recounting a childhood story.

"I still can't believe you're only twenty years old," Coriander marveled, taking another appreciative sip. He didn't recognize the label on the wine, but its well-aged quality was undeniable. "I always imagined fairies as timeless, immortal beings."

"We are…" Shyne hesitated, making a so-so gesture with his hand. "…but new fey are born all the time, and the elders pass on to the Timeless Forest when their time comes."

"Is this even something you should be telling me?" Coriander asked, his curiosity piqued.

Shyne shrugged, a playful glint in his eyes. "Probably not. But I trust you."

"Now, you mentioned coming from the Summer Court. Are there courts for Spring, Autumn, or Winter?"

"Only Summer and Winter," Shyne explained with a sigh. "Summer rules from the spring equinox to the autumn equinox, while Winter governs the rest of the year."

Coriander pondered this for a moment, sipping his wine thoughtfully. "Does that mean you'll have to leave when the equinox arrives?"

"Yes." Shyne's tone was resolute, a hint of inevitability in his voice. "It's a rule as old as the seasons themselves."

Coriander's heart sank as Shyne confirmed the inevitable. He had known their time together was limited, but hearing it aloud made the reality hit harder. The thought of returning to his life without Shyne by his side left an ache he couldn't quite name.

They fell into a contemplative silence. The equinox was less than two weeks away, a looming reminder of the temporary nature of their time together.

Coriander had thoroughly enjoyed the past few weeks. Although he felt ready to return home, Shyne had assured him that the doppelganger had everything in order. There was no need to rush.

The dragonflies that had once danced merrily around them now seemed to flit more cautiously, their delicate wings buzzing with an underlying tension. Even the waterfall's once soothing murmur seemed to echo the heaviness that had settled between them.

"So," Coriander said, trying to keep his voice light and cheerful, "six months isn't that long to wait to see you again."

Shyne didn't immediately respond. Instead, he gently withdrew his arm from around Coriander's shoulders and turned away, a shadow of sadness crossing his face.

"Shyne, what's wrong?" Coriander asked, concern threading through his voice.

"Nothing to be concerned about," Shyne replied, his voice soft but firm. He leaned in and placed a tender kiss on Coriander's forehead. "There's something I need to attend to. I'll be back shortly."

His words hung in the air, leaving Coriander with more questions than answers. Shyne stood then, climbing gracefully from the water. His wings fluttered briefly, catching the light before he vanished into the woods.

Coriander watched as Shyne disappeared into the trees, a mix of confusion and longing swirling within him. He reached out, his fingers brushing the water as if trying to hold on to the moment a little longer. They had shared so much in these few weeks, yet there were still parts of Shyne that felt like a mystery, slipping through his grasp like water. The scent of damp earth and blooming water lilies filled the air, mingling with the crisp aroma of the wine, but even these comforts couldn't chase away the unease settling in Coriander's chest.

He sighed, leaning back against the smooth stones at the pond's edge, the warmth of the sun doing little to ease the cold that had crept into his heart.

"I'm telling you," Samuel hissed, "something is wrong with the prince!"

Leon glanced around, ensuring no one else was in the hallway. Better safe than sorry, he ushered the servant into the nearby study. The room was unused currently, but well kept.

Shutting the door silently, the knight turned to Samuel with a stern look. "You are making very serious accusations."

Whether the chamberlain missed the warning tone in Leon's voice or simply didn't care, he continued forward anyway. Pointing in the direction of the prince's chambers, his voice crackled just above a whisper. "That is NOT the prince!"

Leon sighed, his gaze narrowing slightly. Samuel felt a cold sweat break out on his brow. How could he possibly convince Leon when he himself barely understood what he had seen? How could he explain the vile things whispered in his ear?

"What makes you believe that?" Leon asked, his voice laced with skepticism.

A flush of embarrassment colored Samuel's cheeks. How could he possibly tell the knight about the vile things whispered in his ear? Admitting to a relationship with the prince, even as casual as theirs was, could be disastrous. But he knew—he was certain—that Coriander would never have said such salacious things to him.

"He's just not acting like himself," Samuel finally spluttered, his voice trembling with uncertainty.

"Listen." Leon's tone was firm, implying this was the last he would hear of it. "The prince is under a lot of stress right now. He's to begin the Iron Crown ceremony in a couple of days, and he will be married on the equinox. Do you understand how much pressure is currently on him?"

Samuel did understand and nodded to show as much. The prince had discussed his fears with Samuel many nights as they lay together. Coriander did not want to marry, but he feared letting down the kingdom if he did not produce an heir.

"Good, then I'll hear no more about it," Leon said, missing the trepidation in Samuel's eyes. "Back to your duties. I'm certain the prince will be a little more like himself again soon." Leon tried to put all the assurance he could into those words. Truth be told, Coriander should have returned by now, and he too was already tired of this doppelganger. Maybe it had all the memories of the prince, but it was quickly beginning to act like a royal pain in the ass.

The study was dimly lit, dust motes dancing in the narrow beams of sunlight that slipped through the heavy curtains. The scent of old parchment and polished wood filled the air, adding to the weight of the conversation. Leon opened the door, letting the chamberlain out ahead of him. Samuel gathered the bedding he had set down, his hands trembling slightly. The weight of Leon's dismissal hung heavy in his chest as they departed in different directions.

Not long after, Samuel found himself at the prince's door. He hesitated, his heart pounding in his chest as he hovered near the knocker. Every instinct screamed at him to turn and run, to leave whatever was behind that door alone. But he couldn't—he had to know. Steeling himself, he took a deep breath and grasped the knocker with sweaty palms.

The thing calling itself Coriander answered, and Samuel entered.

As Samuel stepped into the room, a chill ran down his spine. The air felt thick, almost oppressive, as if it were closing in around him. The flickering firelight cast long, twisted shadows that danced along the walls, adding to the sense that something was terribly wrong.

It was sprawled on the bed, posed on its side with a glass of wine casually dangling from one hand. The liquid inside sloshed lazily, as if even the wine was under its dark spell. A predatory smile stretched across its face, too wide and unnatural, as its nude form shamelessly displayed its excitement. The air around it seemed to hum with a dark, unnatural energy. As it raised its other hand toward him, a lone butterfly fluttered into the air and out the window.

"If it isn't my sexy little servant," the thing purred, the words slithering from its lips like a snake through the grass. "I've missed our little... chats." The way it lingered on the last word sent a shiver down Samuel's spine, the familiar phrase twisted into something sinister.

Impossibly, its smile seemed to grow—a smile that never touched its eyes. With a crook of one finger, it beckoned him in further.

The door settled closed behind him with a soft click, sealing him inside the room. Samuel swallowed, his throat dry with fear. He was alone with it now, trapped in the lion's den, with no one to hear him if he screamed.

Coriander found Shyne in the glade where he normally went to meditate. The fairy sat illuminated in the golden shafts of light that broke through the canopy, his arms outstretched and his legs crossed. Butterflies swarmed the clearing, their delicate wings catching the light as they fluttered around him. Several had come to rest along his arms and head, adding to the ethereal sight.

The scent of damp earth and wildflowers filled the air, mingling with the faint aroma of sun-warmed pine. The only sounds were the distant rustling of leaves and the soft, rhythmic breathing of the forest around them.

"I'm sorry if I said something to upset you," the prince said, sitting down across from Shyne and taking up a similar position.

One of Shyne's eyes cracked open slightly, the bright green pupil unfocused but pointed in Coriander's direction. "You didn't." His voice was dream-like, distant, as if coming from another world. "A moment, please."

His eye fluttered closed again. Shyne's breathing slowed and steadied, becoming rhythmic and deep. A few whispers in the Fey language slipped between his lips, and all at once, the butterflies resting on his body took flight to join the rest of the swarm. The air was filled with the soft rustle of wings as they fluttered away in different directions.

Coriander watched in awe, marveling at the connection Shyne seemed to have with the creatures. He knew the fairy had a special bond with the natural world, but he had never seen so many butterflies at once. As the last of them disappeared into the trees, Coriander finally lowered his gaze to see Shyne smiling at him warmly.

"What?" Coriander asked, his heart still racing from the sight.

"You just had such a dreamy look on your face. It was cute." Shyne's voice was gentle, and his words sent a rush of warmth through Coriander, making him blush. But before he could find the right words to respond, Shyne's expression fell, and he sighed heavily. "Cory, you know I can't lie to you, right? Like, literally. Fairies cannot lie."

Coriander hesitated, sensing the seriousness in Shyne's tone. "That's what I've read, and what you've told me. But I don't actually know the truth of it."

Shyne nodded, his eyes searching Coriander's face. "It is true," he emphasized, "but I understand your trepidation." He reached out and took the prince's hands in his, his touch warm and reassuring. "On the solstice, I must return to the Feylands."

"I understand, and I know it'll be a long wait, but—"

"No." Shyne interrupted, his voice firm yet tinged with sorrow. "You don't understand because you don't know everything."

Coriander squeezed his hands, his heart tightening in his chest. "Then tell me," he pleaded in a whisper. "We can figure it out together."

Shyne looked at him for a long moment, the weight of his words heavy in the air between them. He wanted to believe Coriander, to hold on to the hope in his eyes, but he knew what he had to say would change everything.

"By fairy law, we can only come to this world every score of years." He watched as the realization dawned on Coriander's face. The prince drew a sharp breath, his eyes widening slightly in shock.

"Twenty years?!" Coriander's voice was filled with alarm, the words catching in his throat. "When you leave on the equinox, you can't return for twenty years?"

Shyne hung his head low, nodding with a barely perceptible movement as his vision blurred slightly. The pain in Coriander's voice cut through him, and for a moment, he couldn't bring himself to speak. Coriander seemed to have lost his words, his mouth opening and closing as he sputtered out mostly sounds.

"Twenty years..." the prince finally whispered, the enormity of the time sinking in.

"You can come with me," Shyne said, his voice steady, though his eyes betrayed the fear that Coriander would refuse. "There is a way for us to be together."

Coriander froze, his entire world suddenly narrowing down to Shyne's words. He didn't move, didn't even breathe for a moment. Shyne squeezed his hands warmly, trying to offer some comfort.

"There is a flower in the Feylands, crystalline and beautiful. If I bring it to you, and you accept it, I can take you to the Feylands with me."

Lost for words yet again, Coriander studied the man before him. Small tears still clung to the corners of Shyne's eyes, but they still sparkled with hope. The weight of the decision pressed down on him, and he struggled to find his voice. "Does this mean I won't be able to return for twenty years too?"

"No." Shyne replied weakly, looking away again. When he spoke next, his voice was barely a whisper, and it broke with emotion. "You would never be able to return again."

For a long moment, neither of them spoke. The golden light that had bathed the glade seemed to dim, as if the sun itself mourned the words being spoken. A cool breeze whispered through the trees, carrying with it a sense of foreboding that made Coriander's skin prickle. The finality of Shyne's words hung in the air, heavy and suffocating.

Coriander felt as though the ground had been pulled from beneath him, his world tilting on its axis. He searched Shyne's eyes for some sign that this wasn't true, that there was another way. But all he found was sorrow, mirrored in his own.

Chapter Twenty Nine

"You're right, that isn't the prince."

The admission weighed heavily on Leon, stirring a mix of frustration and concern. He had always prided himself on protecting Coriander, but now he felt like he had failed in the worst way. Time was running out, and he had no choice but to trust Samuel if Coriander did.

Samuel responded by swiftly retrieving a small, cheap iron serving spoon—the kind the kitchen used for food preparation—from his belt. In a surprisingly quick motion that caught the well-trained knight off guard, the chamberlain pressed the cold utensil against Leon's forearm.

Nothing happened.

"Ooookayyyy," Leon said hesitantly, slowly pulling his arm away. "Satisfied?"
Samuel's tense expression softened slightly, and he tucked the spoon back into his belt. "Had to be certain," he replied unapologetically, offering a small shrug.

Leon glanced down at the faint indentation the spoon had left on his skin, then raised an eyebrow. "What do you know?"

"Only guesses," Samuel admitted. "The prince hasn't acted like himself since you brought him back from the woods after the bandit attack that cost you your eye."

Leon barely restrained himself from reaching up to touch the eye patch, irritation flickering across his face before he composed himself. Samuel, absorbed in his thoughts, didn't notice.

"He's been rude, entitled, and..." Samuel's face flushed as he continued, "...very forward."

Leon nodded, his mind racing. "Why the spoon?"

"Not long ago, the prince delved into numerous books about fairies. Many of them still clutter his desk even now. While cleaning his quarters, I've often flipped through these volumes. I'm not a very good reader, but certain details caught my attention. Most notably, fairies are harmed by iron."

"And why would you think this has something to do with fairies?" Leon asked, narrowing his eyes.

"When we had the visitor from the desert kingdom, the prince was attacked by a red-haired man. I managed to chase him off with the fire poker because whenever it touched his skin, it burned him. Then, when he leapt from the window, he just seemed to vanish. It all seemed to fit with the prince's research into fairies. Plus," he added hesitantly, as if he didn't want to admit what he was about to say, "the wings."

"The wings?"

Samuel nodded. "While the prince and the stranger were...tangled together, the red-haired man had wings like a dragonfly on his back."

Leon took a moment to survey the unused study, its shelves burdened with dusty tomes and forgotten relics. The flickering light from a nearby candle cast long shadows across the room, and the air was thick with the scent of old parchment. The study, usually a place of quiet contemplation, now felt oppressive, as if the walls themselves were closing in on them. He gauged his next words carefully, striving to maintain authority without casting blame.

"And you didn't report this assault?" Leon asked, his tone firm but measured.

"In his...unwell state, the prince begged me not to," Samuel said, his eyes dropping to the floor, shame creeping into his voice.

"Yeah, that would have caused a lot more problems if you had," Leon replied, his tone softening as he considered the implications.

Samuel looked up, surprised. He had expected a reprimand, at minimum. However, the knight was still regarding him grimly, his expression unreadable.

"Like I said, that isn't the prince in there. It's fairy magic masquerading as the prince." Leon's voice dropped to a whisper, laden with the weight of the revelation. "Coriander was gravely injured by one of the bandits. I had to leave him in the care of the fairy until he recovered."

"What!?" Samuel's voice dripped with anger, his hands balling into fists. The idea that the real prince had been abandoned, left in the care of a creature from myth, was almost too much to bear. "How could you..."

"Calm down, Samuel," Leon interrupted, placing a hand on the servant's shoulder. It was meant to be reassuring, but Samuel flinched at the touch. Leon quickly pulled his hand back, an apology on his lips. He had forgotten the trauma the chamberlain had suffered at the hands of the castle guard. Samuel took a deep breath and waved away the apology, though his expression remained tight with anger.

"I didn't have much choice," Leon continued, his voice tinged with desperation. "The injury was severe, and Coriander likely wouldn't have survived the trip to get him help."

"So instead," Samuel's voice was calmer now, but still carried a razor's edge, "you left him with that creature?"

Leon's jaw tightened, his protective instincts flaring. "I'm not debating that," he responded curtly, "because we have bigger problems. Coriander should have returned by now, and if he's not back before the start of..."

"The Iron Crown!" Samuel interrupted with a gasp, his eyes widening in realization. The name alone carried a weight that few could truly comprehend. He could almost picture it now—the cold, ancient metal resting atop the imposter's head, undoing all the lies in an instant. But at what cost?

Leon could see the understanding dawning in the servant's gaze. He nodded grimly. "If that crown touches the imposter prince's head, the magic will be undone. But I can't leave the castle at the moment, which is why I came to you."

The cold night air didn't seem to touch him. The water embraced his body like a lover's touch, perfectly warm, a stark contrast to the chill in the air. Coriander suspected fairy magic at work, and he didn't mind one bit. He glanced down at the sleeping figure cuddled up against him, highlighted in the pale moonlight.

Shyne's offer earlier in the day still weighed heavily on his mind and continued to chase sleep away. To live eternally with the fairy in the Feylands?

It was an enticing concept, one that clashed heavily with his sense of duty. After all, he had an entire kingdom that would one day rely on him. The thought of abandoning his duty gnawed at Coriander's conscience, a relentless whisper of guilt that grew louder with each passing moment.

A soft murmur escaped Shyne's lips as Coriander shifted, the gentle ripple of water against his skin amplifying the stillness around them. The air was thick with the scent of wet earth and leaves, and every breath he took felt like an invitation to linger in this moment just a little longer. He leaned back and stared at the bright three-quarter moon, his eyes pleading with the celestial body for answers.

But no answers came. Instead, he listened to the quiet call of the few insects still active this late into the year, their songs mingling with the rustling leaves in the distance.

Could he truly abandon his duty to the kingdom? He was his father's only heir, and a broken line of succession could lead to infighting between the noble houses. Such a thing hadn't happened in generations—not since Coriander's several-times-great-grandfather. The resulting civil war of that time nearly tore the young kingdom apart.

Could he walk away, knowing that would likely be the outcome again? The idea of staying, of locking himself into a future dictated by tradition, felt like a slow suffocation. But the pull of Shyne's offer, the chance to escape and live a life free from the chains of responsibility, was almost too tempting to resist.

These thoughts swirled over and over in his mind, chasing sleep away. The waves of his heart, tumultuous and yearning, crashed relentlessly against the steadfast shore of his duty. Each surge of emotion broke upon the unyielding rocks, their force met with unwavering resolve, as love and responsibility waged their timeless battle.

As the cool breeze whispered through the trees, carrying the faint scent of pine, Coriander's mind snapped back to the present. The weight of Shyne's offer hung heavy on his chest, pressing down with the force of a decision he wasn't ready to make.

He was broken from his thoughts as Shyne sat up in a rush, his green eyes seeming to glow with their own inner light as he scanned the darkness.

"Wh…" Coriander began, but Shyne shushed him.

The fairy took a deep breath and spoke a few words in the song-like language of the Fey. As he released the breath, the air around them seemed to hum with energy, the words hanging like notes from a forgotten song. The waters of the pond rippled out from him, and a dense fog began to rise from the water's surface. It billowed up and spread outward into the surrounding forest, swirling with a subtle glow that hinted at the power beneath the surface.

Almost as if in response, Coriander heard the distant neigh of a horse.

"This will keep us hidden," Shyne hissed, "but you must remain silent." Coriander nodded that he understood.

Another neigh sounded closer, accompanied by the sound of crunching underbrush. Whoever it was, they were coming down the deer path from the hills.

"What if it's Leon?" Coriander whispered with barely a sound.

Shyne glared at him, and silently mouthed the words, "It's not," before putting a finger to his lips to reprimand the prince.

A shape began to form through the fog, resolving into a man on a horse. The fog curled around the figure, making it difficult to discern any details. The iron rod in the rider's hand glinted in the moonlight, a stark reminder that danger was never far behind.

For a few moments, Coriander worried the horse might plunge into the pond, unable to see the water, but it miraculously turned away just before it reached the reeds and continued along the edge of the pond.

As the horse and rider finally came close enough to make out, Shyne's hand clamped over his mouth before he could speak.

Samuel sat atop Zedd, scanning the fog with clear frustration etched into the lines of his face. In his left hand, he held the reins tightly, but in his right was a slender rod of iron.

Coriander struggled against Shyne's grasp but could not break free. The fairy's strength was unworldly.

"I am so sorry." The soft whisper in the prince's ear sent chills down his spine.

Coriander twisted enough to glare into Shyne's eyes, bright and wet as they were. He had no voice, but he screamed in his mind to be released.

Shyne closed his eyes for a moment with a heavy breath, the barely held tears finally overflowing their dam and streaking down his cheeks. His breath hitched as he fought to hold back the sobs that threatened to escape, knowing that each tear was another nail in the coffin of what they had shared. As his eyes fluttered back open, they conveyed his despair as he…let the prince go.

Splashing free of his grasp, Coriander climbed to the bank and whirled toward the fairy. His body shook with anger, but his voice was hard and clear. "What the fuck, Shyne?"

Samuel rose in the saddle, looking around. "Cory?" he called to the fog, his eyes still not finding the prince even though they were only a few feet from one another.

Shyne stared at him with forlorn eyes, wordless and breathless, before finally raising one hand and flicking his wrist. Coriander felt the thick soup of magic about them vanish, and the fog began to dissipate immediately.

"Cory!" Samuel shouted, his eyes finally focusing on the prince. He leaped from the saddle, his boots squelching in the mud as he landed. A few quick steps and Samuel was embracing him in a tight hug. Then it seemed a sudden thought struck him, and he released the prince while taking a step back. His eyes stayed firmly on the prince's, and his cheeks colored a deep red. "Cory... You're naked?"

It had the inflection of a confused question, and Coriander couldn't help but laugh. Before he could answer to explain, Zedd nudged his shoulder with a happy whine. Coriander scratched the horse's nose affectionately.

Water splashed as Shyne rose to make for the shore, but Samuel spun and pointed the iron rod in his direction. "Don't you move," Samuel growled, and Shyne complied. He seemed to freeze in place with a supernatural stillness.

"What are you doing here, Sam, and how did you even know where to find me?"

Without lowering the rod, the chamberlain looked at the prince. "Leon sent me. Your wedding is in eight days."

Coriander blinked. Of all the things he expected to hear, this hadn't even been on the list. "My what!?" He sputtered. He didn't even allow Samuel to answer, instead turning a glare to Shyne. "You knew about this?"

Shyne didn't speak. Not even a ripple spread from his body as still as he stood. The only indication he wasn't a statue was the buildup of glistening tears in his eyes. To Coriander, that silence was deafening and more than enough of an answer.

"'*Everything is fine at the castle,*'" Coriander quoted with a shake of his head. "'*Your double had it handled.*' Not really a lie, I suppose, since you can't lie. But that is definitely some twisted truth." He was practically growling now, even as the tears began to flow down Shyne's face. "Why?"

A stuttering breath slid from Shyne's lips as he whispered, "I didn't want to lose you."

The words struck the prince's heart like a dagger, but he steeled himself against the pain. "You may have just done so."

Without another word, Coriander retrieved his pack from the rocks and pulled out his clothes. He hadn't actually looked at them in weeks and was shocked to find them clean and mended. It was almost as if the bandit attack had never happened. He dressed quickly, slinging the rest of his gear on his back. Without even a glance at Shyne, he climbed into Zedd's saddle and offered Samuel a hand up.

Once the chamberlain was seated, they turned, and he ushered Zedd back down the path to the hills. Just before they would have completely disappeared from sight, Coriander spared one final glance behind them.

The pond was empty, a single thin ripple marring its surface, as if the world itself were mourning what had just transpired. Coriander's heart ached with the finality of his choice, each step away from the water's edge feeling like a step into an unknown future. He spared one last glance behind him, but the past, like the ripple, was already fading into memory.

Chapter Thirty

Samuel turned back to them, smiling brightly as a veritable cloud of butterflies scrambled out through the open window. He placed the iron rod down on the desk with careful reverence and proclaimed, "It's finally over."

The princely doppelganger hadn't been too agreeable about leaving, its form shifting and flickering with an unsettling energy as it resisted. Coriander had felt a cold knot of fear in his stomach as the room seemed to hold its breath. But it hadn't expected Samuel's strike. With a single decisive movement, Samuel brought the iron rod down, and the doppelganger's form shattered like fragile glass, releasing the cloud of butterflies into the morning light.

The butterflies danced on the breeze, their delicate wings catching the light like fragments of a shattered dream. The air was filled with a soft, fluttering sound as they rushed toward freedom, their vibrant colors—a swirling blend of blues, yellows, and oranges—standing in stark contrast to the cold iron lying still on the desk. Each flutter seemed to pull a thread of tension from the room, unraveling the fear and uncertainty that had hung so heavily moments before.

As the last of the butterflies fluttered out into the morning, a heavy silence settled over the room. The morning light poured through the open window, casting long shadows across the stone floor. The room, once filled with tension, now felt oddly empty, save for the faint scent of iron and the lingering sense of something unfinished.

Coriander watched the butterflies disappear, his heart heavy with a strange mix of relief and regret. He knew it had to be done, but the sight of the fragile creatures fleeing into the morning left him with an aching emptiness he couldn't quite explain. The doppelganger had been more than just a threat; it had been a mirror, reflecting the doubts and insecurities he tried so hard to suppress. As the butterflies vanished into the open sky, he felt as though he were losing a part of himself—a part that he hadn't yet come to terms with.

Leon gripped his shoulder with a firm, steady hand, his expression softening as he sensed the turmoil beneath Coriander's calm exterior. "We'll get through this," he said, his voice a quiet anchor in the whirlwind of Coriander's thoughts. "But first, let's get you ready to meet your future bride." The knight's smile was forced, but his eyes held a quiet determination—a promise that

Coriander wasn't sure he deserved, but one he was grateful for nonetheless.

Coriander managed a weak smile in return, feeling the weight of the moment settle on him. The doppelganger was gone, but its absence left behind a void that the looming responsibilities could not fill. As the last butterfly vanished from sight, Coriander couldn't help but wonder what this meant for the path ahead. The shadows the doppelganger had cast still lingered in his mind, and he knew that whatever came next, he would have to confront not only the challenges before him but also the ones within.

"No! No! No!" Lady Miranda practically screamed as the florist began unloading the flowers for the ceremony. Coriander, watching from a distance, felt a familiar weariness creeping in. The iron crown ceremony was tomorrow, and she was obsessing over every small detail. It was exhausting.

He didn't even know this woman, yet he was expected to marry her and spend the rest of his life with her. She was beautiful, certainly, but there was no attraction—no connection to this practical stranger. Especially with the way she treated the staff.

"These were supposed to be red roses!" she insisted, her voice sharp enough to cut through the air.

"With respect, ma'am, that isn't the order I received." The florist pulled out a folded piece of paper from his pocket and handed it to her. Lady Miranda snatched it from him and opened it. "Is that not your signature and seal?"

Coriander's curiosity got the better of him, and he approached the scene. The situation was absurd, yet something about it intrigued him. Carefully picking up one of the bundles of flowers, he freed them from the protective paper covering them... and froze.

"It is," Lady Miranda muttered, "but I did not order red clematis!"

Coriander stared at the deep crimson petals, their softness at odds with the sharpness of the scene. The flowers were beautiful, but they were not what anyone had expected. Much like his own life, they were a reminder that not everything went according to plan. And before he could stop himself, laughter bubbled up from his chest. It was the kind of laughter that came from sheer disbelief, and the indignant glare from Lady Miranda only made it worse.

Her fury turned back to the florist. "Take these back and bring roses like I wanted!"

The florist began to sputter a response, something about not having enough time, but Coriander got his laughing under control and interrupted. "These will be fine."

Lady Miranda turned to him, ready to argue, but he stepped forward and took her hands in his. For a moment, she looked as though she might continue, but Coriander's calm, unwavering gaze gave her pause.

"In life, we are rarely granted that which we want," he said, his voice gentle but with an underlying firmness. "It's better to enjoy what we have." He offered her his best dazzling smile, hoping to ease the tension, but his eyes drifted back to the bundle of clematis on the table. Surely, this was no coincidence—a sign that even the best-laid plans could unravel in the face of reality.

Lady Miranda hesitated, her fury simmering just beneath the surface, but eventually, she let out a resigned sigh. "Very well," she said quietly, though her tone made it clear she was far from pleased.

Coriander released her hands, his smile fading as she turned away. He couldn't shake the feeling that the mistake with the flowers was more than just a simple error—it felt like a symbol of his own growing dissatisfaction. This was the woman he was meant to call his queen? The thought of a lifetime spent in her shadow felt like a prison sentence, one that no crown or title could make bearable.

As Lady Miranda moved to inspect the rest of the preparations, Coriander remained by the table, his fingers brushing lightly against the clematis. The flowers were a small consolation, but they were a reminder that life rarely gave what one asked for. The roses Lady Miranda demanded were predictable, controlled—just like the life Coriander was expected to lead. But the clematis, with its wild, twisting vines and deep red petals, spoke of something different, something unplanned and untamed. Perhaps it was time he started asking for something different.

As Coriander finished his vows, the court page lowered the iron crown onto his head. The weight of it felt heavy, a cold and unyielding reminder of the responsibilities that lay ahead. He turned a brief glance to Miranda as the crowd burst into applause. She wore an elegant gown, a masterpiece of ivory lace and delicate frills, clinging to her form with an ethereal grace. Her hair, woven into intricate braids, framed the iron crown that sat perfectly atop her head. The crown was nearly a twin of his own—slightly smaller, thinner, and less ornate.

Another thing that would change when he became king. Not the ceremony exactly, but the subtle signs embedded in many traditions that seemed to label women as inferior.

Next, Samuel approached, dressed in finery that a man of his station would not normally have had access to. Coriander had chosen him for this ceremony and made certain he was properly attired. Honestly, the sight of him in such fine clothes toyed with Coriander's thoughts to the point where he had to adjust his sitting position to hide his interest.

Samuel knelt between the two small thrones temporarily set up in the hall. He held up a pillow between them, and on it sat a small white plate trimmed in gold, holding two small candies.

They were expected to feed them to each other—a show of mutual respect and responsibility, an oath to care for one another.

Coriander lifted his piece and held it out for Lady Miranda. As she leaned forward, her lips barely parted, Coriander couldn't help but wonder what she would think if she knew the memories that haunted him in that moment. She opened her lips just slightly, and he placed the candy on her tongue. She sat back, chewing slowly, the sweetness evident in her eyes and smile. For a moment, her gaze flickered with something unreadable—was it concern? Understanding? Did she sense the turmoil that churned beneath his composed exterior?

She picked up her piece and offered it to him in the same manner. As she placed it on his tongue, Coriander sat back, beginning to chew and...

...Warm summer heat enveloped him, the air thick with the heady scent of blooming flowers and the musk of desire. The taste of sweet nectar lingered on his lips as fingers traced patterns of fire along his skin, each touch igniting a fresh wave of pleasure. Bodies together, writhing in rhythm. Hot skin pressed together, fingers and lips exploring sensitive areas...

He nearly let a moan escape his lips but managed to stifle it, disguising it as a sigh of appreciation for the sweetness of the candy. He pressed one arm across his lap in an attempt to control the other signs of his desire.

That was most definitely fairy food, he thought. Certainly a memory of him and Shyne together, as the food they made was created from their memories. First the flowers, and now this. Shyne was trying to win him back, and the worst part? It was working.

As the memory faded, Coriander struggled to regain his composure. The iron crown, cold and heavy on his brow, felt like a chain binding him to the throne—a stark contrast to the warmth and freedom he had known with Shyne. How could he rule a kingdom when part of him yearned for a life that was anything but conventional? Despite the not-quite-lies and manipulations of the man, Coriander found himself missing him greatly. Yes, the sex was otherworldly, but Shyne himself was kind, compassionate, and caring.

He knew the dangers of distraction—how one wrong move could unravel everything he'd worked for, how the court would seize on any sign of weakness. Yet, as the memory of Shyne's touch lingered, Coriander couldn't help but wonder if the real danger was in denying his heart entirely.

Finally, Coriander's body calmed down enough that by the time he stood to bow to the crowd, his 'stiffness' wasn't obvious. The applause echoed through the hall, but to Coriander, it felt distant, like the sound of a dream fading into the morning light. As he met Miranda's eyes once more, her smile remained poised, but there was a flicker of something in her gaze that made him pause. Was she, too, performing her own role in this grand theater of courtly life, masking her true feelings behind a practiced facade?

As the warmth of the fire lulled him into a hazy calm, Coriander's mind raced. Was this what he wanted? Or had he simply sought comfort in the easiest way he knew how? The iron crown on his head, the applause of the crowd, the expectations of the kingdom—all of it seemed to pale in comparison to the memory of Shyne's touch.

As the applause died down and the crowd's gaze followed him, Coriander forced a smile, knowing that beneath the surface, the battle between duty and desire had only just begun.

Nothing unusual happened the next day during the silver crown ceremony. Coriander was almost ready to believe that Shyne had given up on his antics, but deep down, he knew better.

So, when it came time to open presents during the gold crown ceremony, Coriander wasn't too surprised when a large, ornately decorated box suddenly burst open, releasing thousands of butterflies. As he lifted the lid, a hush fell over the room. His heart beat just a little faster, sensing that something unusual was about to happen. And then, with a rush of color and motion, the butterflies filled the hall like a living tapestry, their wings shimmering in the candlelight.

The air in the hall seemed to change as the butterflies filled it—lighter, more fragrant, as if the scent of blooming flowers had been carried in on their wings. The warm glow of the candlelight softened, refracted through the myriad colors of the butterflies, casting a kaleidoscope of hues on the walls and the faces of the onlookers. For a moment, it was as if the entire hall had been transported to another world, one woven from magic and dreams.

The butterflies fluttered gracefully, some drifting toward the flower arrangements, their delicate forms contrasting beautifully against the vibrant blooms, while others found their way out through the open windows, carrying with them the whispers of magic. The structured elegance of the crown ceremony was suddenly infused with a wild, unpredictable energy, as if the very essence of the event had been turned on its head.

Lady Miranda gasped in delight, her eyes widening with childlike wonder as the butterflies swirled around her. The sight left her positively glowing, her laughter ringing through the hall like a melody. The lords and ladies exchanged excited whispers, their faces alight with the shared enchantment of the moment. Yet, beneath her joy, a flicker of curiosity remained: Who had sent such a magnificent gift, and what did it really mean?

But when the box was examined, there was no note, no sign of who had sent it. Lady Miranda's curiosity was piqued, but even as she questioned the attendants, no answers were found. The mystery only added to the allure of the evening, leaving everyone wondering who could have orchestrated such an enchanting spectacle.

Coriander couldn't help but smile as he watched the display, though a part of him remained guarded. As the butterflies danced around him, he felt a flicker of something deeper—an emotion he couldn't quite place. There was awe, yes, but also a sense of longing, as if the magic stirred memories from another time, another place. Shyne's touch was unmistakable, and with it came the bittersweet reminder of all that had been lost and all that remained uncertain.

But why now? Coriander wondered, his thoughts swirling as the butterflies did. Shyne had always been unpredictable, but this—this felt like more than just a playful display. Was it a message, a reminder, or perhaps a warning cloaked in beauty? The questions gnawed at him, even as he forced a smile for the lords and ladies around him.

As the last of the butterflies fluttered out of sight, Coriander felt a chill that had nothing to do with the cool night air. The magic was beautiful, yes, but it was also a reminder—a sign that Shyne was still watching, still playing his games. And if Coriander knew anything about Shyne, it was that this was only the beginning.

This was sure to be a day that would be remembered for a long time in the kingdom.

Coriander stood in the pale moonlight streaming in from his window, the cool late fall air brushing his skin and raising goosebumps. After his time in the woods, the city air smelled foul—stale with the weight of responsibilities and unspoken expectations. Tomorrow was the wedding, the event that loomed over him like a specter, demanding a decision he wasn't ready to make. The thought of it tightened in his chest, a cage that seemed to close in around him. Was this really what he wanted? Or was he simply bowing to the pressures that had always dictated his life?

Faintly, he heard the door to his room open and close softly, followed by the quiet clink of dishes as Samuel set the tray on the table. The scent of freshly baked bread and spiced wine mingled with the crispness of the night air, grounding him in the present.

"Having second thoughts?" Samuel's voice was soft-spoken as he moved to stand beside the prince. He grasped Coriander's arm gently, just below the silken sleeve of his nightshirt, his touch warm against Coriander's cool skin.

Coriander grunted in response, his thoughts too tangled to form a clear answer. Loyalty to the kingdom, or loyalty to his heart? The question gnawed at him, its answer eluding him as he stood on the precipice of a choice that would change everything. If he followed his heart, he would be defying centuries of tradition, risking not only his future but the stability of the kingdom. Yet, the thought of living a life not chosen by him, of being bound to someone he didn't love, made his chest ache with a hollowness he couldn't bear.

Samuel's hand slid down his arm, and their fingers intertwined. The touch was steady—an anchor in the storm of Coriander's thoughts. Samuel leaned forward and pressed a soft kiss on the prince's cheek.

"He wanted me to go away with him forever."

Samuel squeezed his hand, his gaze flickering briefly to the moonlit window, then back to Coriander, his eyes filled with a mixture of concern and something deeper—something he couldn't quite bring himself to voice. "I, of course, don't want to see you go." His voice was somber but steady. "But I'll stand by whatever you choose. It's your happiness that matters most to me, even if it means..." He let the words hang in the air, unfinished but understood.

Coriander turned to Samuel, his eyes shining with moonlight and sparkling with barely contained tears. "If only it were so simple," he murmured, his voice catching in his throat. The pull of duty was a heavy chain around his heart, but the desire to follow his own path, to listen to the voice of his heart, was equally strong.

Samuel leaned against the prince, pressing their bodies together. "It is," he whispered breathlessly as he pressed their lips together. Coriander's resolve faltered as Samuel's lips met his, a gentle, breathless whisper of a kiss that spoke of longing and a bittersweet farewell. For a heartbeat, he let himself fall into it, into the warmth and the comfort it offered, even as the shadow of tomorrow loomed over them.

As the city bells tolled, the band struck up the traditional wedding march. Coriander turned, Leon at his side, to watch as Lady Miranda began her walk down the aisle between the rows of attending nobles.

She moved with grace, stepping gingerly behind the young girl spreading flower petals in front of her. Her dress was an extravagant affair, with layers of silk and lace spilling down her body like a fountain. Her face was veiled, as was the tradition, and a sparkling tiara adorned her brow.

Even Coriander had to admit, the sight was breathtaking.

The grand hall was adorned with garlands of red clematis and golden ribbons, the air thick with the scent of blooming flowers and the murmur of anticipation. Nobles sat in their finest attire, their eyes fixed on the bride as she glided forward, every step echoing on the marble floor. The candles lining the aisle flickered gently, casting a soft glow, but to Coriander, the light seemed to dim around him, as if the shadows were creeping in.

The music stopped as she reached his side, and the priest began the wedding sermon. Coriander was hardly listening, his mind on other things. Every word from the priest felt like a nail sealing his fate, each phrase a reminder of the life he was expected to lead. Duty. Honor. Tradition. They weighed on him like a cloak of iron, suffocating the part of him that yearned for something different, something wild and untamed.

The evening bells meant the start of the ceremony, but also that there were still several hours until midnight. With a swift enough horse, maybe even Zedd, he could make...

"I do." Lady Miranda's voice startled him from his thoughts. The priest began to repeat the oath, stopping at the appropriate moment for Coriander's answer.

"I do," he answered automatically, but his voice was hesitant. He could tell the priest had heard the tone, and even Lady Miranda's veil shifted slightly, although he could not see her expression. Leon stood rigid beside him, a shadow of concern passing over his features. His eyes flickered to Coriander, a silent question hanging in the air. Reluctantly, Leon stepped between them, holding a royal red pillow with two golden rings atop it.

Lady Miranda took the larger band and, almost grasping his hand forcefully, slid the ring onto his third finger.

He picked up the other band, staring at it for what felt like an eternity. He could hear whispers breaking out from the attending nobles. Coriander's hand trembled as he reached for the ring. His fingers felt like lead as he lifted it, each movement a struggle against the invisible chains holding him back. His heart pounded louder with every passing second, drowning out the murmurs of the crowd. The weight of the golden band felt heavy in his palm, a shackle more than a promise. He hesitated, staring at it as if it held all the answers he was too afraid to seek. The memory of the stranger's green eyes haunted him, a constant reminder of his growing uncertainty. The stranger's eyes, full of mystery and promise—this wasn't the future they had shown him.

With a deep breath, he took her hand and slid the ring into place.

"You may now kiss the bride!" the priest exclaimed.

Coriander took hold of the veil, his hand unsteady and hesitant. His heart raced and pounded in his ears, and he could feel the sweat building on his skin. A gentle tug pulled the veil free of its bindings.

His fingers were unsteady as they grasped the delicate fabric. For a fleeting moment, he swore he saw red hair and green eyes gazing back at him, a vision so vivid it sent a jolt through his chest. The world around him blurred, the candlelight turning into a haze. But as the veil slipped away, reality snapped back into place. Miranda stood before him, her rusty brown hair barely visible beneath her head covering, her dark eyes a mixture of confusion and concern.

"I...I..." Coriander began stuttering. Then he steeled himself. "I can't do this."

Panic surged through him, tightening his chest like a vise. This wasn't right. He wasn't ready. He couldn't go through with it. An inexplicable force urged him to run, to break free from the gilded cage closing in around him. His gaze darted to the grand doors, the only path to freedom, and without another thought, he turned on his heel.

The crowd gasped and began to chatter loudly. Faces blurred into a sea of shocked expressions, mouths moving in a flurry of whispered accusations and questions. Somewhere, a woman sobbed, the sound piercing the air like a knife, but it was all drowned out by the shout of his father.

"Guards! Stop him!"

"Coriander," Leon whispered urgently, his voice barely audible over the rising din. "What are you doing?"

Coriander tried to push through the two men that stepped in front of him as he approached the doors. Despite his struggles, they overpowered him quickly.

"No!" he cried out, continuing to struggle in their grips. "I must go! There isn't time!"

"Restrain him!" his father's voice cut through the noise like a blade, cold and unyielding. "The prince will learn the price of disobedience."

Coriander fought against the guards' grip, his body thrashing in a frenzy of panic. The crowd's gasps and whispers became a distant roar in his ears. He had to get out. He had to find Shyne. This wasn't how it was supposed to end. He shouted, his voice cracking with the force of his desperation, but the heavy doors swung shut, silencing his pleas as they locked him away from the world beyond.

Even as the heavy doors closed, the assembled room could hear the desperate shouts of the prince as he was carried off.

Shyne stood at the water's edge, the crystalline flower still clutched in his hand. He knew he was being foolish. He had hurt the prince, wounded him with his accursed fairy ways. It wasn't something he could change; deceit was woven into his very being, as natural and immutable as the passing of seasons. To be Fey was to be truthfully deceitful.

His sigh escaped in a cloud of steam, mingling with the cold night air. He could feel winter's power pressing against him, clawing at his skin, ready to tear him apart if he overstayed his welcome in its domain.

"Oh, poor sweet *Summer* child." The voice was the breath of Winter itself, a chill that sent ice down his spine. He froze, panic seizing him. This was impossible. It wasn't yet the solstice; she shouldn't be here!

The air thickened, turning so cold that each breath he drew burned like fire. Frost crackled at his feet, spreading outwards in jagged lines, consuming the warmth with an insatiable hunger. The water at his toes crystallized, freezing in an instant under the weight of her presence.

Delicate arms, pale as death and tipped with nails of onyx, encircled him from behind. Her touch was like a thousand needles piercing his flesh, leaving behind trails of blood red welts. Cold seeped into every joint, an unyielding force, just like her croaking yet melodic voice that echoed in the stillness.

"How very wistful. To fall in love with a mortal?"

"You cannot be here." Shyne's voice was sharp, defiant. This was still Summer's time, if only for a heartbeat longer.

Her voice shifted, a symphony of cracking ice and falling snow. "Do not dare presume what the Queen of Winter can or cannot do, child." It softened, each word a whisper of snowflakes settling on a frozen landscape. "Join my court, Shyne of Clematis. Gain more time with your mortal prince."

The offer slid into his mind like a blade of ice, sharp and alluring. It wasn't just an invitation—it was a promise of eternity, a chance to escape the fleeting nature of life. For a heartbeat, he considered it, the thought of endless time with Coriander tempting him more than he would ever admit. But to become part of her court, to surrender to the cold, the darkness—he couldn't.

She sensed his refusal even before he could voice it. Her arms withdrew, and a whispered "Pity..." lingered in the air before a gale of freezing wind exploded around him. It tore at his skin, the force of it pushing him back, yet she remained unseen. Only the glittering frost on the trees and ground marked her presence, like a scar left by the claws of some ancient beast.

Cold sank into his marrow, gnawing at his warmth, his life. The very shadows seemed to writhe with her disappointment, stretching long fingers towards him, ready to pull him into the void of eternal night. Shyne felt his resolve wavering, his thoughts clouding as if the frost was creeping into his mind.

But he resisted, clinging to the last vestiges of warmth within him. As he stepped into the water, the crystalline flower slipped from his grasp. It shattered upon the ground, the sound like delicate glass breaking. The tiny shards scattered, catching the moonlight one last time before a gust of unseen wind swept them away into the night, leaving no trace of what had been.

Epilogue

The door to the king's chambers opened, and the man entered, greeted by happy shouts of "Father!" from the two young children as they rushed to meet him. He scooped up both the boy and the girl, holding them close as they giggled in delight. As he held them, a wave of warmth filled him, mingled with a bittersweet twinge of nostalgia. He had chosen this path—father, king, husband—but some days, the ghosts of what could have been whispered at the edges of his happiness.

"You are home early," the children's mother said, setting down the book she was reading and rising from the chair. Her eyes sparkled as she straightened her evening robe and approached her husband.

"Yes! I finished the summit early and had enough time to make it back today. I nearly stopped at an inn for the night, but the approaching storm turned, so I was able to continue on." He set the still-giggling children down and embraced his wife. "My queen." He gave a little bow before planting a soft kiss on her cheek.

She smiled at the affection, though Coriander noticed the slight tightening of her grip on his arm. "I just summoned the steward to come and take the children to bed. He should be along in a moment."

As if on cue, someone knocked at the door behind the king. He turned and opened it.

"King Coriander!" the steward exclaimed in surprise. He had also been unaware of the king's early return.

"Samuel!" Coriander's tone was jovial, and he gripped the steward's arm with familiarity. When their eyes met, a silent understanding passed between them, a look that lasted just a heartbeat longer than necessary. Then, with a subtle smile, Coriander released him, his fingertips gently sliding down the length of Samuel's arm. The room felt suddenly smaller, the air thick with unspoken words.

Miranda stepped forward, sliding her arm through Coriander's with a grace that spoke of practiced composure. "Samuel." Her voice was calm, but the brief flicker in her eyes spoke of a thousand questions. "Please take the children to bed."

"Yes, Queen Miranda." He took the children by their hands. "Come now, Leon and Sara. Time for bed." He began to lead them from the room amid much complaining.

"Will you tell us a story?" little Leon asked the steward.

Samuel chuckled softly, glancing back at the king for a brief moment before turning to the children. "How about a fairy tale?" His voice carried a note of wistfulness, a quiet acknowledgment of the stories that had once bound them all in a different kind of magic.

As Samuel led the children away, Coriander watched him go, a pang of something indefinable tightening in his chest. The past lingered like a shadow in the candlelight, even as the present unfolded in front of him—warm, bright, and full of complexities he was only beginning to understand.

Coriander turned to his wife. Even twenty years later, she was still beautiful, with only a few fine wrinkles around her eyes to mark the passage of time. Though it had been a challenge in the beginning, he had grown to love her in many ways. They had found a steady companionship, a kind of love born from shared trials and quiet understanding. Yet, in the recesses of his heart, he sometimes wondered if there was a part of him that she could never truly reach—a part that belonged to another time, another place.

"I know I just got back, my love, but I have some work to finish in the study. I'll be to bed later."

The queen softly giggled. "I suspected as much," she said, giving him a playful push towards the door. "Don't let Samuel keep you up too late."

He laughed, and just as he was about to return her playful jab, something caught his eye. A faint glimmer from the window. His breath hitched. Was that...? No. It couldn't be. His mind struggled to make sense of it. Had it been real, or just a trick of the light? For a split second, his heart raced with the old, familiar thrill of possibility, stirring memories he had long thought buried.

Outside, a gentle breeze rustled the curtains, drawing Coriander's gaze back to the window. On the other side, hidden in the shadows, Shyne held his breath.

Giant fingers wrapped around the edge of the sill, one finger dangerously close to him. Shyne held onto the small splinter of wood underneath, barely the size of a ladybug. He had let his emotions get the better of him and had accidentally allowed his red glow to emerge for just a moment. Or maybe he had wanted to do it, deep down, a silent cry for the attention of the man he had once known.

Either way, he was nearly certain the prince—the KING—had seen.

After a few moments, the hands reached for the shutters and closed them. Shyne sighed in relief, letting his glow fade as he pushed off from the window sill. His wings buzzed, catching the wind, carrying him away from the life he could never be a part of. As he flew, the world blurred around him—a dark, endless expanse. And for a fleeting moment, he allowed himself to wish things could have been different.

He had been back in the world for a few nights, and had used that time to catch up on what had passed in his absence. Seeing Coriander now, older, a king with a family, was like a knife to his heart. Twenty years had passed, and yet the sight of him still made Shyne's pulse quicken. He had thought he could move on, forget. But deep down, he knew he never would.

He passed by the newest statue in the courtyard, erected nearly a decade ago. It depicted an armored knight, his custom helm partially covering one eye. Shyne had read the plaque at the base several times now:

"High Commander Knight Leon: Gone from the world, but remembered as its hero."

The statue stood tall in the courtyard, a silent sentinel that had witnessed the passage of time. It was a tribute to a hero, a friend, a man who had stood at Coriander's side through so much. Shyne felt a pang of guilt every time he looked at it, a reminder of the paths they had all taken—the paths that had led them here, to this place of quiet solitude and unspoken regrets.

Coriander's father had gone to war with the desert kingdom. The campaign had been bloody and had lasted for many years. The knight had lost his life defending a village on the border. He had held out until the civilians had evacuated but fell just before reinforcements had arrived.

Coriander's father had passed a few years later, and the newly crowned king had brought an end to the war. He was signing a peace agreement even as his son was being born back home. His daughter came a few years later.

The countryside blew past beneath him. It was nearly no time at all before he reached the tiny forest where his pond lay. Almost all the land around had been cleared, converted to farmland with a few scattered villages nearby. However, a small area of woods had been left, by decree of the king, that his pond still sat at the heart of.

Shyne circled the area a few times before making his decision. From this high up, he could almost see the city on the horizon.

He dove. The air whistled around him as he spiraled downward. Despite his speed, the water barely rippled as he vanished below its surface. At least until the few tiny droplets of water that followed him hit its surface.

In the quiet of the pond, he found solace. Yet, as he settled into the familiar darkness, the echoes of a life not lived whispered to him, a reminder that some wounds, no matter how deep beneath the surface, never truly heal.

Printed in Great Britain
by Amazon